# In the Seasons of War

Aubrie Sandness

Raemichael— Puyallup, Washington
ISBN: 979-8-218-53647-3
eBook ISBN: 979-8-3305-4638-1
Library of Congress Control Number: 2024924009
Title: *In the Seasons of War*
Author: Aubrie Sandness
Digital distribution | 2024
Paperback | 2024

This is a work of fiction. The characters, names, incidents, places, and dialogue are products of the author's imagination, and are not to be construed as real.

# Dedication

I would like to dedicate this book to first and foremost my husband. Brandon, when I came to you and told you I wanted to write a book, without hesitating you encouraged me to do so. You are my biggest supporter. You believed in me when I didn't believe in myself, and to my two beautiful children, I hope you both know how much I love you and that you can achieve your dreams at any age. There is no time limit. Believe in yourself and find someone who believes in me as much as your dad does. Lastly, to my parents, you guys have been there for me all my life. Never questioned or doubted my goals. Always encouraging myself and my brothers to be the best we can be. Thank you all so much for supporting my dreams. I love you all.

# Chapter One
Saoirse

It had been 1,826 days since the war began. I couldn't even remember what silence sounded like. The constant screams and sounds of bombs exploding all hours of the day made you forget the little things in life, like just how beautiful silence can be.

These few months sitting here in this prison cell had given me that silence that I had longed for but had forgot its existence. Oddly, even in my current situation I found this all sort of comforting. A sense of comfort that I hadn't felt in the last five years since the war broke out. Hitler's reign and terror grew rapidly and at a much quicker pace than anyone could have imagined. Then before we knew it, he invaded Poland and so began one of the worst wars in our history.

Fast forward to now and I have found myself sitting in a prison cell, bloodied, and beaten. Our hospital had been seized by Nazi SS soldiers. Hitler's worst of them when it came to his regime. They were making their way through the countryside, only a few of them, but it was enough to kill every sick, wounded man, woman and child in our sector hospital. Including the wounded soldiers we had been treating. London, when the war broke out, created 12 sectors in and outside the city limits.

The major hospitals in the city treated those with severe wounds caused from the Nazi air raids. Once they had been stable to move, we would transport them to the remaining sector hospitals outside the city to make their full recovery, creating more room for the hospitals in London.

I was matron nurse of my hospital; I was also a part of helping to transport those from one sector to the next when needed. We had made this trek over a thousand times without incident. But that day, was the day it all would be different. Many of my fellow friends, that doctors and nurses had been killed. Why they decided to take myself and some of other nurses as hostages and not kill us right then and there was something I was a question I was not willing or more so wanting to have answered. I knew that whatever was to come was going to be far worse than having been killed and my body left there lifeless and rotting in the earth.

As for now, all I could do was shut my eyes and dream of Aiden and the life we had before. His beautiful face and charming smile, the sound of his voice when he called my name and the comforting way he would hold me. I could see his face now so clearly as if he was here lying next to me. I rolled over to my side hugging myself tightly, keeping our memories alive in my head. Which brought me just enough comfort the drift off to sleep.

My name is Saoirse, Saoirse Dunn. I am the Matron Nurse at Saint Giles Hospital in London. I have been the Matron Nurse there since 1932. All my life I wanted to make a difference and help those in need. I went to nursing school in Belgium, The Berkendael Medical Institute, received my nursing diploma and from there went on to be a Matron Nurse at Saint Giles Hospital.

Saint Giles Hospital was a beautiful place in the Southwark of London, England. It had been an infirmary during World War 1. I was honored to have been able to work there and be with my dear friend Abby who was also a nurse at Saint Giles. Oh, how we were so full of hope and love. Eager to go out into this world and make a name for us.

I was born in Galway, Ireland. My father, Calvin Dunn, was a prestigious doctor who worked in Dublin. He was well renowned, a man who broke down barriers in his field. After the Great War of 1917, my father had realized the doctors were overwhelmed with performing all their doctoral duties on their own, and while we had women in the field helping us, they were under educated when it came to performing some medical tasked. He took it upon himself to educate those outside his field in an article he wrote of the importance in having female led nurses in the medical industry.

He would be one of the first set of doctors who had begun taking women under their wing and teaching them how to be a nurse. Like for example, how to draw blood, suture wounds, administrate morphine, take vitals the works. He knew the importance of their roles and the trust that was needed to work together efficiently in this environment. His article was published in the newspapers all around Ireland. His words had a ripple effect in the medical industry encouraging all those who wanted to work in the medical field to apply to the nursing program and upon finishing their education they would start their training in the field.

He was very influential and because of his persistence, the nurse field was born. He became one of the most profound Doctors Dublin ever had. It was also there while training several nurses he met my mother.

Grace Donavan. An Intelligent, witty, and beautiful young woman who yearned to help those in need. She spoke 3 different languages, German, Spanish and French. My mother was born in Galway to two loving parents.

She had dreamed of making a difference in this world. She had a gentle soul and a kindred spirit, people gravitated towards her so willingly. She always helped those in need as much as she could. And when the opportunity came up for her to go to nursing school, she could not pass up the opportunity. Her parents, beyond proud, helped her pack up her things and set her up in an apartment in Dublin near her college where she would be performing her studies over the next few years.

Her first day at Saint Patrick's Hospital she was ecstatic. A little nervous, but excited none the less. Eager to excel, she was top of her class and stood out among all the other nurses. She was given the head Matron Nurse job at Saint Patrick's and that there was where my father had met her. He always describes to me how my mother lit up every room she walked in. She excelled in everything that she did. Executing her nurse tasked perfectly.

The knowledge she had acquired was beyond what any other nurses had learned in school. She took it upon herself to learn beyond her nurse duties which put her in a position to perform surgical procedures with her fellow doctors. She was exquisite he would tell me. Her long dark brown hair, big brown eyes, but not just any pair of brown eyes, he would tell me. Her eyes were a deep shade of brown that when the sun hit them, they held a beautiful color of gold flakes that almost turned them hazel, and when she smiled her eyes smiled too and your whole world froze in time when she looked at you.

He couldn't keep his eyes off her not for one second. My father, who was tall with broad shoulders, and dark brown hair, had the most beautiful blue eyes that lit up with his smile. He made her feel like she was the only person in the room every time he would look at her. She said it was love at first sight when they met.

My parents had developed a close friendship and over the next couple of years. Getting to know one another, that friendship bond which grew into an ever-enduring love. Wasn't long after my dad had begun courting my mother that he had asked her to marry him.

She, without hesitation, said yes. She would always joke at how long it took my father to ask her to be his wife. Patience, she said was the one thing she had when it came to my father. As he was a man of over-thinking and taking ones time as for, he thought he wasn't good enough for her. Once he came to his silly senses and realized he was the man for my mother, they then were married shortly thereafter.

They moved from Dublin to Galway, buying a small home they would commute to and from several days during the week traveling by train to and from Dublin. My parents were the reason I become a nurse. Their inspiration for all the good they had both accomplished over the years was a legacy I wanted for my own. One I was proud to join and contribute to in their names.

They were rewarded for their incredible humanitarian aid efforts around Galway, Dublin and even traveling abroad to foreign countries attending to the sick and elderly and giving medical aid to those in need.

A foundation was set up in their names to help fund the education for those who wanted to become nurses and doctors alike but were unable to afford to do so. All the while having myself and my twin brother Calloway in tow. Our life was always full of adventure.

Around the time we turned 10, we had moved from Galway and headed off to London, England. Our mother and father were asked to expand their teachings in London. For the remainder of my youth and into my adult years, London had become our home and that there is where I met him, Aiden Dean Palo.

# Chapter Two
## Aiden

"Captain Palo! Captain Palo! Aiden get the fuck up. They are dropping bombs on us. Hurry up, get moving." Jimmy was yelling at all the other soldiers to move out and move fast.

"We need to retreat and move towards the tree line take cover from the all the gun fire." Sergeant Nance began to climb out of a foxhole when suddenly an artillery shell landed next to him. A loud bang rang through my ears as I flew backwards.

Captain Nance hurled into the sky, his body parts blown to bits as one part of him went flying in one direction and the other half of him landing just my left side. Dirt, blood and bone covered my body and face. My eyes burned from the powder and debris caused from the explosion, making everything blurry for a short moment. I waited for my eyes to adjust and then came to my feet.

The shouting and the violent screams of soldiers next to me calling out for their mothers as they lay there dying. I yelled for a medic reassuring some of my men that they were going to be fine. I gave one of my men a shot of morphine from his kit. His stomach had been blown and his intestines were falling out of his side. He was trying to put them back in when I had happened upon him.

Once the morphine had kicked in, his screams stopped and then he was gone. I shut his eyes, grabbed my weapon and started to run. I ran around ordering all my men to take cover in their foxholes until the shelling was done. It seemed as if the shelling was coming from all around me.

I found Jimmy. He had hunkered down in his fox hole; I jumped in next to him covering my head from the debris of the tree branches falling all around us. I closed my eyes and took my mind to anywhere but here. As the sounds began to fade, I was taken back to one of many beautiful memories frozen in time. Our wedding Day.

*December 1944*

*Dear Saoirse,*

*It's 25<sup>th</sup> of December 1944, here in Belgium. My body cold and numb unable to stop the constant shaking caused by winters brutal reign. We are unable to light fires for we don't want to give our positions away so here, I sit in a hole dug out covered in tree branches in this dense forest. Everything is so quiet, no birds or sounds of animals just pure silence. it's been snowing for days since we left our last post.*

*Lately, the days seem merged together, my eyes heavy and weak, rest doesn't come often, but when it does, I find myself dreaming of you. Back in your arms holding you, kissing you. Breathing you in, the smell of your vanilla and sugar perfume the one you love so much. Resting faintly on your skin, so soft so radiant. That kind perfect smile, what I would give to see that smile and those big brown eyes staring back into mine.*

*Entangled in one another without a care in the world. For a moment I have you here, but I know it's just a fever dream. One I hang onto until we are in each other's arms again. I love you my darling Saoirse. I'll be home soon.*

*All my love,*
*Aiden.*

After what seemed like an eternity the shelling finally stopped. Coming back from my escapism and into the present, Jimmy and I climbed out of our foxholes and started to assess the damage that had been done and how many men we had lost today.

Many of the men were wounded, limbs blown off, others having been blown to pieces. Their body parts scattered into pieces. We lost 3 men that day. 4 more were badly injured and were sent to the hospital. The rest seemed fine from the outside, but inside, their minds were collapsing. You learn to bury it; the fear, until you can't control it anymore then one day you find yourself unable to control the fear from all you have seen. Breaking down, your mind suddenly without warning, collapses all at once.

But not in the way one would think. No, there is no screaming, no sudden bouts of rage. It's more quiet and much more subtle. It has an eerie way about it. Your body stiffens as if you're frozen in time. Unable to think, unable to move. You just sit and stare off into the distance. It's like your brain puts you in this catatonic state to protect you from having a nervous breakdown from what you have seen. It's made a name for itself around here, "shell shock" and up until today, I hadn't seen what it looked like. As dawn approached, I sat and stared out into the distant tree line. So far from home and so close to death, I found myself thinking of home once again.

I was born and raised in London, England my father, Armise Palo, was born in Finland and after he graduated secondary school, my father moved to London to attend oxford university. He graduated at the top of his class earning his degree in History.

After graduation, the university had asked him to come on and join their teaching staff. He gladly accepted with no hesitation and so began his tenor as a history professor at Oxford University. He was one of their youngest professors to be employed at just 22 years old. My father was highly intelligent his parents would have loved for him to become a chemist or doctor, but out of his love for historical literature, he chose to be a history professor.

My mother, Charlotte Serrano, Charlie is what she liked to go by, was born in Barcelona, Spain. Her parents were of generational wealth, not sure what they did for a living. Once she met and married my father, they had completely disowned her from the family. They wanted her to marry a man of great wealth and that of a prestigious career. My father was not what they had wanted for their daughter. They made it very clear to her that if she chose him, she was never to be welcomed in their presence nor would she receive any financial support; and without hesitation, my mother chose love over money.

My mother was a sensational ballet dancer. Performing in all the best ballet shows and toured all around the world. She had met my father while holidaying in London over Christmas. The two met at a local pub. It was love at first sight. They became inseparable with one another and after only a few short weeks my father proposed. They got married in a cute little church with my father's family and their friends in attendance.

After a few years of marital bliss, my mother gave birth to me. Growing up there were always adventures we took as a family. Both of my parents believed the best way to learn was to be out in the world experiencing everything it had to offer. Going on long car rides to the coast, visiting historical monuments. My father was an avid reader. He read to me as a baby and well into my early childhood years. From Shakespeare, to Dickens, Tolstoy, and Jane Austen.

My parents were strong believers in supporting all my dreams and endeavors in life. Always making sure I knew their love for me was always unconditional. When I started school, my mother went back to dancing for a little while teaching young children ballet and performance arts. Over the years they had tried to have more children, but my mother having had several miscarriages, was ultimately unable to have any more children.

As an only child I was doted on immensely by my parents, but I had always longed for a sibling to play with. I was a shy child, typically playing alone in school while other children had tons of friends. Until one day a persistent little boy had come up to me and asked to be my friend. Timid and slightly reserved, this little boy sat next to me every day in the school yard. Talking on and on about all things and everything. Until, one day I had asked him why he was here talking to me? he said because you are my friend, and from that day on the two of us were inseparable.

Jimmy was the exact opposite of me, ying to my yang. He was funny, outgoing, girls loved him, he always made them laugh. He was a magnet for attracting people. We were always getting into trouble, always making makeshift of things, running around town after school. Riding our bikes to the pond to go fishing.

Jimmy became like a second son to my parents. He was not only my best friend, but the brother I had longed for.

Jimmy's home life wasn't as loving and caring as mine was. His parents, strict and at times, abusive despised Jimmy and I being friends. They were prejudice and treated all those they thought less of poorly. Jimmy's parents came from an immensely wealthy family. They threw lavish parties, had the most beautiful house.

Traveled the world and would complain about all the poor people and how they shouldn't be allowed to exist in this world. They were vile, hateful human beings. How Jimmy didn't turn out to be like them must have been a fluke in their genetics; thankfully. When he turned 14, Jimmy had gotten in a huge fight with his dad, his dad lashed out violently towards Jimmy.

That fight was the final blow for Jimmy. He had packed up his bag, walked out the front door never to return home again.

Typically, Jimmy never fought back, but this time he did and after his dad had punched him in the face, Jimmy turned around and hit his father right back. Knocking him on his back. Jimmy could have continued to beat him, but instead told his father and mother, that he was done and had enough of being a part of their family. Jimmy packed up all that he could and walked out their door never to return. That night showed up at my house and without hesitation, my parents took him in and raised us up together. They loved him as much as they loved me. Brothers we were born to be.

Graduation came faster than we had imagined it would and after the ceremony, we had decided to head into downtown London with some of our other mates stop at a local pub Michelangelo's, which was often the spot to go in town.

We had just walked in when I had spotted her. The most beautiful girl I had ever laid eyes on. She took my breath away as I watched her from across the bar. I tried not to stare but it was hard not to. Her dark brown hair in bountiful soft curls that draped just over her shoulders, her light sun kissed skin that complimented her olive-green dress she was wearing. Her smile, that beautiful smile of hers lit up the room. I kept my distance and watched her as I contemplated if I should approach her or not. But before I could decide our eyes, just then, had met. They were the most beautiful green eyes I had ever seen, and in that moment, I knew I wasn't leaving here until I knew her name.

# Chapter Three
## Abby

Born in London, England to Rupert and Mary Edwards. Her father Rupert was a bank investor in London's ever growing prominent residences. Her mother Mary also born and raised in London coming from a prominent family. Mary's father, an investor had met Rupert's father on the job and the two had become quick friends. Mary and Rupert had met while attending one of several Fundraising dinners our parents had hosted.

They were forever intertwined with one another and soon after Rupert and Mary had wed, they too would welcome twins of their own. Abby and Henry who were inseparable since birth. They had a deep loving relationship with their parents. Both well educated, kind, smart and equally beautiful and handsome just all-around good kids.

Abby and Saoirse's parents met at a charity event and both girls had instantly hit it off. The two of them attended the same all girls boarding school and eventually attended the same nursing school together as well. Abby always admired Saoirse, her beauty, her kindness, and how intuitive and smart Saoirse was.

***

Saoirse was the bonus sister I never had but always wanted. Callaway, Henry, Saoirse and I were always together. There was a time you wouldn't have seen us all together.

Henry, my twin brother, was special from the day he was born. He broke down the barriers around him. He was artistic, brilliant minded, avid reader. He was never the quiet, or the shy type of guy, always stood up for those when needed and used his voice to say what people would deem "unconventional" in our time.

Our father had always hoped for Henry to take up the family business and become and investor as well, but Henry had dreams of his own that did not involve our father, the family business or any of the shady businessmen our father surrounded himself with. Henry never approved of our father's business dealings. Even though our father agreed with Henry, business is business, and some men are just born evil and obtain it anyway they can he would tell Henry. It was not his job to reprimand or dispel disapproval of how they choose to do business. It was his job to make sure their investments made them money.

Henry, who was stubborn at times, would never see eye to eye with our father, and for that Henry would have no part in that future. This, for some time, caused a wedge between Henry and our father, but in due time our father learned to respect Henry's decisions and chose to support Henry. For him, that was more important than losing a son to a foolish disagreement.

Henry who was a remarkable artist, loved to paint, and draw. He wrote poetry, some of the most beautiful poetry I have ever read. He loved history. Henry devoured knowledge of anything and everything he could get his hands on.  "No matter what they tell you; you can never be too educated," Henry would say.

When Henry and Callaway began a relationship, I and Saoirse were the only ones they could be themselves around. Going on long car rides to the beach, having picnics by the lake, we were always doing something, the four of us. Callaway and Henry had dreams to attend Oxford university together.

They talked about how they would buy a small little cottage just outside of London and live out the rest of their days growing old together. Oh, how we were all dreamers back then, unaware of the devastation the war would bring upon us.

It's funny how life can be so innocent and carefree one second and then suddenly you're fighting for your life and others. None of us knew what was to come, we in this moment never wanted to be anywhere else but here, laughing and full of love without any care in the world.

# Chapter Four
## Saoirse

It was the Summer of 1936, two summers before the war began. Graduation day had come and were eager to head out into the world. Our parents couldn't have been prouder of my brother and I. Myself, who followed in our parents' footsteps, would be attending Saint Giles nursing program, and Callaway would be going to one of the most prestigious art schools in the country, Oxford University.

Abby would be joining me, attending the same nursing program and Henry would join Callaway at Oxford to study History with the intent of becoming a professor. After graduation we all had decided to go out in the city and head to a local pub that several of our classmates would be in attendance. The sound of loud music and laughter echoed from the building as we approached Michelangelo's. This was the place to be.

The heavy smell of a sweet sweaty smell of musk filled the air. Upon entering the pub, the smell hit me like a ton of bricks as we walked through the pubs doors. I looked around taking in all the excitement the environment had to offer. We made our way to the back of the pub and found a table to sit at. The boys had gone and ordered us some beverages.

The night was just getting started, the pub was filled with most of the people we knew. As I was scanning the room, observing all the people, out of the corner of my eye sitting with his mates was a tall, broad-shouldered, dark-haired man, with golden olive skin and the most beautiful light blue eyes I have ever seen.

My eyes locked in on him, I tried to look away and focus my attention elsewhere, but my eyes kept reverting to him. His eyes suddenly caught on to mine and a wave of heat flushed over my entire body. Embarrassed as I was, I couldn't take my eyes off of him nor could he take his off of mine. What seemed to be an eternity but was only for a mere few seconds we were the only two in that room.

I then quickly glanced away, trying to recover from having been caught off guard. I could still feel his gaze on me. I tried not to glance over at him, but I could see him in my peripheral vision as he got up from the bar and made his way toward me. My heart began to rapidly beat at a pace I was unfamiliar with.

Thinking here I am about to have a heart attack because a handsome young man was walking towards me, I started to tell myself, stay calm and breathe. Don't panic Saoirse, just breathe. Abby caught wind of what was happening as she saw this young man walk towards me. Her eyes lit up, her smile giving it away as he approached, he held out his hand.

He introduced himself. "Hello, miss my name is Aiden, Aiden Palo," he smiled.

As he stood there just before me, his smile and handsome physic taking my breath away for a short moment.

I held out my hand and as I took his in mine, I told him my name. "Hello, Aiden. My name is Saoirse, Saoirse Dunn."

Aiden's eyes brightened as if they were smiling on their own. "Wow! That's a beautiful name, I have never seen you all in here before. Are you from around here?" he replied.

"No, we have never been to this pub before. Well myself and my friend Abby here, have not been. But our brothers Calloway and Henry both have," I said back to him.

It was hard to keep my eyes off him. The conversation carried on, introducing himself to each of us, he then invited his friends to come over so he could introduce us all.

"This here is my best mate, Jimmy!" Aiden proudly exclaimed.

Jimmy nodded his head and lifted his hat from his head as he greeted us. "Hello there, ladies," he turned to Henry and Calloway and shook both of their hands.

We all gathered around the table, ordered some more beverages and talked the night away.

This night was like a dream I never wanted it to end.

# Chapter Five
## Saoirse

That night started a whirlwind summer romance for not just Aiden and I but Abby and Jimmy as well. The six of us were inseparable. We spent each waking moment we could with one another. Long summer walks alongside the pond, picnics in the park, some days we would find a shaded tree and sit for hours reading poetry to one another. When the summer nights were coming to an end, we all were able to save up enough money between our summer jobs and found a place just outside of London that we could live in while we attended school.

Aiden and Jimmy maintained their day jobs working down at the market, while I, Abby, Calloway and Henry attended to our studies at our respective schools. Our parents helped us out with our finances until we were done with school and were able to make a living on our own.

Two years into our studies, Abby and I had finished our nursing program. To say we were ecstatic was an understatement. Both of us would be hired on permanently at St. Giles Hospital where we had attended for our nursing program in Southwark, London.

Life was finally falling into place and as the six of us stood in the living room of our house, we knew that this was the beginning of something truly special. We raised our glasses in a toast, celebrating this new chapter in our lives and the adventures that lay ahead.

The next morning as the sun began to rise, the light poured in through the windows casting a warm glow over the room, illuminating my face. As I woke a sense of excitement filled me up with joy, I shot up out of bed and quickly began getting ready for the day.

It was our first day at St. Giles as Matron Nurses. I couldn't contain myself. After months of hard work, we were finally here in this moment. I took a shower and put on my nursing gown and went out to the kitchen, made a pot of coffee and started on breakfast.

Abby came in shortly after I started breakfast and began to make our lunches. The boys were still sleeping from a night of celebration. Trying to stay quiet, not wanting to wake them, I left a note by the fridge and let Aiden know we had made extra food for them all and that I would see him later tonight. I grabbed my jacket and slipped on my shoes. We packed up our lunch in our bookbags and walked out the door heading down to the Hospital.

Walking up the steps through the hospital doors the smell of sanitized floors always made me smile. We were met by a nurse sitting at the front desk. Her name was Martha, she had been working at Saint Giles for a year now. We both waved and said, "Good Morning," as we walked backed to the nurses lounge where we would put our bags and have our lunches and breaks throughout our shifts.

We then made our rounds as we moved from every floor checking in on our patients. Martha, Checking in on us from time to time. Making sure we were both settling in just fine. After we made our rounds, we went to the supply closet and took inventory of all the supplies we had used for the day. Which ones we were low on and would need to be stocked again.  Checking off each patients charts every hour. Giving them their required medications, replacing their IV drips, and cleaning any open wounds and readdressing them with new bandages. Every hour or so, depending on the patients' needs we would be checking it off on their medical charts that they had received the proper care as needed.  go after we have finished up with each new patient. Our day's busy and filled with multiple tasked always made our shifts fly by fast.

Both Abby and I always had a wonderful time with Martha. We had met her during our nursing program. She had often showed us the ropes and helped us with any questions we needed answering. Martha introduced us to Becca, she had started a few months before us, then Rose, Marjorie, Tasha, and Ethel. All coming from different nursing programs around the city before finally getting hired on here at St. Giles Hospital. Us girls all became such quick friends. All so sweet and kind, I couldn't have asked for a more perfect group of nurses to work with.

After our long day had come to an end, Abby and I gathered our things and headed back home. We said goodnight to the other girls and off we all went our separate ways, headed back home to await another day's worth of work. When Abby and I walked through the door, the boys had already made dinner for us. Mashed potatoes with gravy, green beans and carrots, and meatloaf for the main course.

I gave Aiden a kiss, Abby doing the same with Jimmy. All of us sitting around the table enjoying this wonderful meal the boys had cooked. We talked about each other's day, just normal conversation over dinner. Once we were finished, we cleaned up and headed to bed for the night. Happy, but exhausted as we crawled into bed, Aiden and I wrapped up in each other's arms both drifting off into a deep sleep.

Over the next several months as our lives continued as normal, things around us politically were beginning to intensify. I couldn't help but get this sickening sinking feeling in my stomach as I read the morning paper on Germany and what they were doing to the Jewish community.

"I don't get it Aiden; how could anyone just stand by and do nothing for these poor people," I continued. "Look, it said here that neighbors are turning in those that they believe to be of Jewish descent all to save their own homes and jobs. Putting fear in everyone who does not comply with the rules. Turning innocent people in how sickening. As if it's a crime to be Jewish. It's absolutely appalling!"

Aiden took my hand in his. "I know love, but what is it we are supposed to do? It's maddening what's happening, but there isn't much we can do here but hope it doesn't go beyond anything more than what has been done already," Aiden said.

"I guess you are right, but it doesn't feel right. This whole thing, something is about to happen Aiden…I can't shake this feeling of anxiousness I have had lately," I admitted. "The hospitals have begun stocking up on extra medical supplies, we have hired on more nurses. Something tells me that there is a storm coming our way and soon."

Aiden stared off into the distance and took a moment before he said, "You can't stop whatever is coming our way. Whatever is meant to be will be."

We finished our lunch date up and walked over to the boardwalk along the river and my thoughts raced endlessly, but Aiden was right, whatever is coming our way is going to happen regardless. To live in fear of the unknown will only make you or anyone go crazy, and that is no way to live your life in the "what ifs" just live for today.

It was a beautiful sunny day, and the board walk was busy with passersby, Aiden and I love walking around this pond. The swans had their little babies all out on the ponds edge staying close by to their mum's as they mimic their every move. I walked just a little bit ahead of Aiden moving closer to the edge of the ponds watery edge so I could see the little ones and their mum. As I bent down, they would inch a little closer to their mummy's for safety.

"Aw, you precious little ones, I'm not going to hurt you," I smiled as they continued moving down the edge of the grass. I stood up and brushed off any dirt from my dress. When I turned around to call for Aiden, there he was down on one knee holding a box in his hand that displayed a stunning diamond ring inside.

Shaking, he said, "Saoirse, I know we had talked about waiting a little while longer before we would decide on marriage, after we had both saved up some money and have a place of our own…but I realized that no matter how little we have or if we are living with our friends, or are in a home of our own, home is what and where we make it, and my home is wherever I am with you. That's all I care about. From the moment I laid my eyes on you that night in Michelangelo's I knew you were the one I was going to spend the rest of my life with. You are the love of my life, and I can understand if you want to wait, you can say no right here, and I will get up and be happy with the decision you choose. But if you don't mind me asking, you would be Mrs. Saoirse Pal—"

Before he could finish, I blurted out, "Yes, yes, yes. Of course I will marry you! A million times over, yes!"

Aiden got up from his knee and placed the ring on my ring finger. We embraced one another having not yet noticing all the people around us cheering and congratulating us.

Abby, Jimmy, Henry and Calloway had been waiting patiently nearby making sure they wouldn't be seen by me before Aiden had got the chance to make his proposal.

They came running down the hill after I had said yes and embraced us both. Calloway capturing the moment for us with his camera. This day couldn't have been more perfect.

That evening we had phoned our parents of the good news. Aiden had gone to my father and asked for my hand in marriage weeks ago and of course without hesitation my father approved of our betrothal. For they thought the world of Aiden. When I told them the happy news and how Aiden proposed, they were over the moon and joyful for us both. When the weekend had come, we had planned to head to my parents' house for a celebratory engagement dinner. Family, and friends from work were all invited to my parents' house for a wonderful evening.

The night was beyond anything I could have imagined. Laughter echoed throughout the evening. The sound of music played as we all danced and ate our way well into the late evening hours. As the night started to calm down, our friends and family headed home for the night and we said our goodbyes.

Aiden and I walked hand in hand down my parents' long driveway, Aiden twirling me around and the two of us dancing around in circles embracing one another. When our eyes met face to face, I couldn't help to think that this is what dreams are made of. Right here holding me tight as we get lost staring into one another's eyes like we have so many times before. I put my hands to his face and pulled him in close, kissing his lips, breathing in his scent, his hands on my waist, just the two of us here in this moment.

# Chapter Six
## The Planning

The next couple of months flew by in a blur. Aiden and I had started planning our wedding nuptials the day after our engagement party. We both agreed on a backyard wedding at my parents' house as their home was big enough to accommodate all of Aiden's family, as well as mine and our friends' families who would all be in attendance. We had set a date for the end of summer on August 20th.

The summer days would be dying down, heading into fall and the weather would be perfect for an outdoor wedding. It was very important to both Aiden and I to include both of our family traditions within our wedding.

Sprays of Orange Blossoms, roses, lilies and spring Squill would be in abundance within the centerpiece arrangements for all the tables and then they would line the aisle-way as well. My parents had this beautiful tree in their backyard, a lilac tree that would be in full bloom. Making it the backdrop for our alter. We both agreed that my parents and his parents would prepare traditional wedding dishes from both our cultures and my mother would make our wedding cake.

Traditional Irish food would be that of Irish fruit cake made with raisins, currants, sultanas and candied peels, with each layer soaked in Irish whiskey to bring together all those rich flavors. We would have a spread of Tapas, gazpacho and spit roasted meat such as sausage rolls, crisp sandwiches and cocktail sausages, Irish soda bread, mashed potatoes and cabbage. Irish whiskey in abundance of course and a beautiful rendition of Spanish and Irish songs alike playing throughout the evening.

Aiden would be dressed in his traditional Spanish attire, a bright orange tailored suit with a vest to match. As for me, I would be wearing a princess cut dress, classic white in color that pooled around my feet, with a beautiful Irish lace shawl wrapped around my arms and a floral crown made of lavender and wildflowers; my hair would be braided with flowers woven in between my braids and my bouquet would be made up of lavender. For the Irish lavender represents love and devotion and is used commonly throughout Irish weddings.

Abby, my maid of honor, would be wearing a lavender colored lace gown with a wildflower Boquete. Becca was my other bridesmaid. She would be wearing a lavender lace gown to match Abby's with the lace pattern appearing differently on her dress as to not match the Maid of honor and holding a wildflower bouquet as well. Typically, Irish weddings do not have the best man or maid of honor standing up with the bride and groom during the ceremony, but Latin weddings do, and we both agreed that we wanted our closest friends standing with us up at the altar. It wouldn't feel right not having them standing up there with us.

Jimmy, Aiden's best man, would wear a black tailored suit with a vest that matched Aiden's suit, Henry's attire would match Jimmy's and Calloway dressed in an all-black suite with an orange shirt underneath his black vest to match the boys' suites, would be performing our ceremony's nuptials.

Everything was falling right into place, and we could not wait to celebrate our love surrounded by family and friends.

# Chapter Seven
## Our Wedding Day

Today was the day, our wedding day. The summer's sun shined through my old bedroom window as I laid in my bed. I couldn't help rising early with mornings, light feeling giddy after all, it is our wedding day. I sat up and stretched out my arms and legs. The house was still quiet as the hustle and bustle of today's nuptials had not begun just yet.

I could smell the coffee my mum had brewed coming from the kitchen. I stood up and began to head straight for the powder room. I turned the shower on and stepped in.

The warm water hit my face and chest as it soaked every inch of my skin. I stood there for a few minutes allowing my brain to wake up before I grabbed my shampoo bottle and began washing my hair. After I washed out my hair, I grabbed the Lavender and eucalyptus scented soap bar and started to lather it up to form suds and then washed it all over my body and face. I finished washing up and turned the shower off. I grabbed my towel and patted my skin dry. Abby would be here in a short while to do my hair and makeup.

As I entered my bedroom closet, I saw my dress hanging just there in the doorway. I took a moment to admire all the delicate details from my hand sown lace shawl to the gorgeous handcrafted floral crown. Tears of joy began to fall down my face. Knowing in a few short hours I would soon be Mrs. Saoirse Palo.

I wiped the tears from my eyes when I heard Abby's voice down the corridor. "Is the bride to be up and in the shower, because we must be on time for today. My darling, sweet best friend you mustn't be sleeping in and wasting away precious time," Abby said with a chuckle.

"Yes, my dearest sweet Abby I am up and showered," I replied, sarcastically as she walked through the door holding her dress, her makeup bag and all her hair supplies all while juggling a cup of coffee for me.

Abby handed me the cup of coffee; I took it and breathed it in deeply the rich coco bean scent was starting to awaken my soul as I went to take my first sip. "How did you manage to sleep?" Abby asked me.

"I got as much sleep as one could get the day before she gets married," I replied with a smile.

I sat down in the chair and Abby started to dry my hair. She pulled my hair back into a beautiful Dutch braid, intertwining the lavender flowers and placing them delicately throughout my hair.

After my hair was done, she moved on to the makeup. A little bit of eyeliner, mascara some powder all over the face and a soft nude lip. She moved out of the way of the mirror to place my floral crown upon my head.

"You are so beautiful, the most beautiful bride to be," Abby said as tears welled in her eyes.

"Oh, stop you are going to make me cry." I stood up to embrace her. "Only because you are the best and can make anyone beautiful. Thank you, Abby, you did a beautiful job."

My mum then walked in. She put her hands to her face. "Oh, my sweet baby girl, you look so… she took a pause catching her breathe. You look radiant. Abby, darling, you did an exceptional job sweetheart," Mum joyfully said.

"Thank you," Abby exclaimed, walking over to hug my mum.

Moments later, Becca walked in the door. "I'm so sorry I'm running late, you wouldn't believe the chaos at the train station, my goodness…." Becca looked up mid-sentence pausing as she caught a glimpse of me. "Oh my gosh you look remarkable!" she joyful cried out as she dropped her things and came over to hug me.

Having the three most important women in my life standing around me helping me get ready for today, I couldn't have been more blessed. My mum walked over and grabbed my wedding dress hanging from the doorway.

Delicately, they all helped me put my dress on. My mum carefully buttoned every individual button down the spine of my dress. Once it was all done and smoothed out, a collective gasp and awes filled the room.

"Stop it, you are all going to make me cry and then I'm going to ruin this gorgeous makeup Abby has done for me," I said to them waving them off holding back all my tears of joy.

Abby grabbed my floral bouquet and placed it in my hands. I looked at her. "You know, soon enough you will be here standing before me. Only then, I will be placing your wedding bouquet within your hands," I said to Abby.

Abby sighed with a smile. "Yes, if only Jimmy would be so quick to propose. I love that man to pieces but he sure does love to take his sweet time when it comes to, well anything in life. Especially a wedding proposal," Abby said with her sarcastic eye rolls and the smirk, she had on her face.

As I was about to respond, I heard Jimmy coming down the hallway. Knocking on the doorframe, making his presence known confirming it was okay to enter the room. "Well, my sweet darling that might just happen soon enough," he came waltzing in and took Abby in his arms, giving her a big ole kiss.

Abby, of course, playfully pushed Jimmy off her and said, "Jimmy darling, we are in the middle of getting ready, and you should be with Aiden getting him up and ready, along with Henry and Calloway."

Jimmy flirtatiously replied, "Well alrighty than, I'll get right on that my wee lass."

Abby smiled back, shooing him off. "Go on my darling love, get to it. You know we can't have you all be late for the nuptials and once you are done getting dressed, I am going to need you all see to it that make you all make yourselves useful and go help with the last bit of set up," Abby said, smirking at Jimmy.

Just before Jimmy headed on out, he gave Abby one last kiss and replied, "Of course my darling love, anything for you, my fiery angel." Abby kissed Jimmy back as he headed out to get Aiden, Calloway and Henry.

"Men," Abby said with an eye roll as we all laughed out loud hysterically. "What am I going to do with that boy?" Abby chuckled.

"Well, he clearly loves you no doubt about that, and you love and adore him. Jimmy is just patient and in no rush. He will propose soon enough I guarantee," I said to Abby.

"I know, I just hope it's soon, seeing you and Aiden getting married gets me all excited for when I finally get to walk down the aisle and can't help to think about when or if it will even happen," Abby said as I helped her button her dress.

"I know love, but just give him some more time it will happen soon enough. The man adores you. He might be slightly crazy, but no doubt he is crazy in love with you," I said as she turned around.

We both hugged one another tight, then we helped Becca with her hair and makeup and helped slip on Becca's dress.

As the three of us stood in the mirror holding our bouquets, my mum, standing nearby had unbeknownst to us, taken our photo. The three of us stood together in front of the mirror, staring back at each other's reflections, smiles on our faces. A moment frozen in time to be remembered for eternity.

***

"Get up, get up, get up!" Jimmy exclaimed with excitement as he was jumping on me. "It's your wedding day mate!"

I shoved him off me all the while laughing as he fell to the floor. Grinning ear to ear, I couldn't help but exude the same excitement he had for me today. "Jimmy, I can't believe today is the day," I continued, "Marrying the girl of my dreams, I didn't even think that was possible."

"Yeah, I didn't think it was going to happen either," Jimmy chimed in sarcastically. "No, in all honesty, she is perfect mate. I mean she puts up with your crazy ass of course. She is the perfect girl just for you and I am sincerely happy for you," Jimmy said with a big smile on his face before bringing me in for a hug. "I have already woken Henry and Calloway up. They will be here in a few short moments showered and dressed, and we will then toast to today's blessing and ceremonial tidings."

A short moment later Henry and Calloway both walked into the room. "Looking sharp mates," I said as they waltzed in tugging at their suites and ties.

"You ready for today my soon to be brother-in-law?" Calloway asked as he gave me a hug.

"I couldn't be more ready; I have been waiting for this day since the moment I met Saoirse," I said back to him.

We then poured four shot glasses full of Irish whiskey toasting to today's blessings and to Saoirse and Aiden's wonderful future together. Once the toast was made, we all tossed back our shots. Slamming the glasses down on the bedstand. The four of us hugged one another then Henry and Calloway made their way to the backyard to finish up with setting up the chairs so the flowers could be spread down the aisleway.

Jimmy, with his charming smile, stood with me a few moments

longer when he pulled out a ring from his pocket and looked at me. Staring at the ring then looking back at Jimmy I knew exactly what he was thinking. Before the words came out of his mouth, I said to him, "I hope you plan on using that tonight because I fear it's beginning to burn a hole in your pocket and with that comes the potential loss of the ring."

Holding the ring in his hand and then looking back at me, Jimmy replied, "I know, I know. I just hope I'm the right one for her. I don't come from money. I'm not nearly as smart as she is. I have been told I will amount to nothing more times than I can count. And here I have the most amazing girl and I fear I will never be able to give her the life she deserves."

"Jimmy," I said to him. "You can't be that blind. The way Abby looks at you she adores you, mate. Every chance she gets, she makes it clear to you and all of us that she is more than ready for you to propose. She loves you more than life itself and you would be foolish to think otherwise. Ask her and ask her tonight, I know you didn't bring that ring here for it to just sit in your pocket. With my blessing I beg you to please ask for her hand in marriage, because mate I am done taking care of your crazy ass," I said laughing as I shook his shoulder trying to break him from his self-pity thoughts.

"You are right, I'm going to propose to her tonight. She is the girl of my dreams, and I am ready to spend my life with her. No more waiting!" he exclaimed, happily as we embraced one another. "Thanks mate, for everything you're a real one you know that," Jimmy said to me.

"Yeah, I know you are too, now let's go get us our brides," I said to him as we both walked out the room to our new beginnings.

***

The time had come as I stood in the Corridor hidden from the crowd waiting patiently for everyone to take their seats.

"You nervous?" Abby asked me.

"No, I'm more ready than ever," I said, smiling back at her.

The music began to play a beautiful Irish melody. Aiden already standing at the Alter, watching as my mum and Calloway walked down the aisle together first, then Abby and Jimmy and Becca and Henry.

Once everyone was in their place, I came around the corner arm in arm with my father. The guest all rose as I made my way down the aisle. I glanced around. So many familiar faces and as I made my way through the crowd, suddenly meeting my eyes with Aiden' as they always do. I tried to contain my emotions; I couldn't help but feel the tears start to well up as I approached him with the biggest smile on my face.

My father placed my hand in his as Calloway asked, "Who gives this bride away?"

"I do," my father replied.

Never wavering from each other's gaze, taking his hand in mind, I stood next to him, and all my fears and anxiety disappeared.

My breaths steady, my heart begins to ease and descend to its normal rhythm. The love in the room was palpable as the ceremony began with playful jokes and the story of how we met. Standing before our families and friends who are all in attendance, their laughter's filling the air and their tears of joy as their cheers echoed throughout the ceremony watching us exchange our vows and our promises to one another. Marking the ceremony to a close as we said our "I do's" and sealed our love with an eternal kiss, both knowing our love would last a lifetime.

The reception followed, filled with music, lots and lots of food an abundance of toasts, and the unforgettable memories that would be made. Aiden whispered in my ear while we danced our first dance, "Don't tell Abby, but Jimmy is planning on proposing to her tonight."

I took my head off his shoulder beaming with joy, smiling ear to ear. "She's going to be so thrilled. She thought he was never going to propose," I smiled, holding Aiden's gaze.

"Looks like we are all going to get our happily ever after once and for all." Pulling me in closer, Aiden rested our heads together.

I replied, "Yes, looks to be that way after all."

Aiden put his hands to my face and gave me a gentle kiss as our song came to its end.

We headed back to our table and grabbed some food, mingled with our guests and took photos throughout the evening, as the night was just beginning to die down.

Most of our family and friends had left by now. My parents and Abby's parents were inside brewing a pot of coffee, reminiscing about all the wonderful moments from today. Aiden, I, Abby, Jimmy, Henry, Calloway and Becca were all sitting out by the patio quietly listening to the music, relaxing and enjoying the last of what would be these final summer's warm nights as fall would soon to be approaching.

Jimmy stood and turned to take Abby's hand. "Would you mind having this dance with me."

Abby and I looked at each other both smirking.

"Yes of course you may." Abby giggled as she took Jimmy's hand and the two walked off into the night.

A few short moments later, I heard a high pitch squeal, looking to our left Abby and Jimmy were embracing one another kissing and hugging. She came running over. Without the ability to contain her excitement, she blurted out, "We are engaged!" Abby exclaimed.
She held out her hand showing us her stunning ring. Congratulating both Jimmy and Abby, we all embraced the tow of them ending our beautiful evening in the most perfect way.

# Chapter Eight
September

It was nearly two weeks of marital bliss when our lives were drastically turned upside down. The news broke, spread across all newsstands and across radio airwaves that on September 1st, 1939, Germany had invaded Poland. Just two days later, England and France among several other countries, would declare war on Germany. What seemed to be words fallen on deaf ears, was a reality none of us were ready to accept. Time had seemed to have stopped, as the weight of the news had started to settle upon us, and the world as we knew it was about to change forever.

Aiden, I, Abby, Jimmy, Callaway, and Henry sat in our living room in silence as we listened while our Prime Minister delivered a speech of resilience and patriotism over the radio. He encouraged we prepared ourselves with food, water, candles anything we could gather in abundance. Then just before his speech was to commence, he said it there, right there as clear as day, "All and every able-bodied young man your services would be needed. If you are willing, I encourage you all to report to your local military base to enlist as we will need each one of you to win this war," Prime Minister finished.

My heart sank into my stomach as I reached for Aiden's hand, squeezing it tightly. My eyes caught Abby's as we exchanged a look, words left unspoken, for we both knew exactly, what the other was thinking. As soon as the radio went silent, there for a moment you could hear a pin drop. All of us trying to comprehend what was about to unfold in the coming days, months or even years. My brain having a hard time accepting what was said.

Without hesitation Aiden, Jimmy, Henry and Callaway stood up from the couches and went to their rooms to begin gathering their things. "Aiden!" I shouted, as I followed him to our bedroom tears filling my eyes trying to grab a hold of my senses.

"You don't have to do this, just wait a second maybe we heard him wrong, maybe you should wait until they give us further information? Can you just stop for a second, please! Aiden look at me?" I exclaimed as I grabbed Aiden by his arm, hoping he would stop and come to his sense. Aiden turned around slowly dropping his bag on our bed walked over to me. He put his hands gently on my face, looking straight into my eyes, as tears streamed down my face, I grabbed his hands as he kissed my forehead and then kissed my mouth, taking a deep breath in and placing our heads together, letting out a deep sigh. "We both know how this is going to go. I can't just sit by and do nothing. Our prime minster has asked those who are able to fight to stand up for our country and fight. I wouldn't be a man if I let everyone else go and I stayed here. Believe me, I don't want to go, I'm scared shitless right now, the thought of being away from you while all of this will all be happening scares me more than I can put into words, But I must go, and I must fight," Aiden said.

Tears fell from our faces as we embraced one another. Both fearing this would be the last time holding one another. We stood there silent, for a few moments, "I heard what you are saying, I know I can't change your mind, I won't change your mind, I'm just scared of losing you, but I know this is what you have to do," I replied.

I held on to him tighter than I have ever done before. After several more minutes I began to help him pack up his bag. Not knowing exactly what he can take, he packed a few pieces of clothing and a picture of me. We set his bag by the door, that night at dinner the tone was that of a somber feeling. We hardly touched our food. When it came time to retreat to our bedrooms, I wasn't ready for the night to come to an end. For in the morning time, Abby and I would be saying goodbye to our loved ones.

Aiden and I made love several times that night, unable to sleep, thoughts of the unknown, no doubt were running rampant through both our minds. Making the most of the last few hours we had before daylight. We focused on what we had, which was each other.

The morning light started to shine through our curtain windows, still lying there in our bed, intertwined with one another tracing my fingers over every inch of Aiden's face. My eyes following my fingers as they moved from his hairline at the top of his forehead, all the way down his temple towards his ears to his jaw-line, up to eyes, over his nose and down to his lips. Photographing all of him to memory, as I leaned in and kissed his lips. Shortly thereafter, we both knew it was time to get up.

The birds outside beginning to harmonize with the rising sun, singing their melodies, I remember thinking how it must be nice being blissfully unaware of what may come. We both headed to shower, my thighs sore from the night before, but still longing for his touch and gentle kisses on my skin as he held my body close to his.

After our shower we got dressed as the others were waking up, I made everyone breakfast and put the kettle on. Knowing this was going to be our last breakfast together for a while, I prepared eggs benedict with hollandaise sauce and freshly squeezed orange juice and a fruit bowl for everyone. Once they were all finished eating, we cleaned up gathered their things and we headed downtown.

It is a short walk into the city, the recruit office was easy to spot as the line of young men alike wrapped around the block. I squeezed Aiden's arm, nervous and anxious for him, and for all the young men here. They were boys most of them, nearly 17, I presume eager to go off into battle. We stood just a little bit from the line and said our goodbyes to one another.

"Calloway, stay out of trouble please, and make it back home to me, mum and father. Don't do anything stupid. I would never hear the end of it if something were to happen to you," I giggled as I embraced him. "Be safe and act smart." Calloway smiled at me as he went on to Hug Abby and say his goodbyes.

"Jimmy, you hear that? you don't go making yourself a hero either! After all, you still need to come home and marry me," Abby said with a smile holding back tears. Jimmy pulled her in close, "I mean it don't do anything foolish. I need you back here with me, you understand?" Jimmy smirking back at her, "You are quite the spit fire this morning my darling…" Jimmy said.

"Jimmy, I mean it stop playing around," Abby interrupted him.

"I promise you I will fight hard to make my way back to you my darling love, and soon I will make an honest woman out of you, I promise," Jimmy said, then he kissed Abby's forehead and lips, grabbing his bag and went to stand with Calloway.

"Henry, you and Calloway watch over one another. Be safe and be smart out there, I love you Henry," Abby said, Hugging Henry before he went and joined Jimmy and Calloway in line.

"Well," I let out a sigh, "I don't think I need to repeat what Abby said, But I will kill you myself if you pull any stupid stunts," I said with a half-smile patting his chest, fixing his shirt collar.

Aiden pulled me in close as I wrapped my arms around him, "Please, please come back to me, don't leave me here to live in this life without you. It's us together, in this world or…. there is no or, just us and nothing else," I said as I held onto him a moment longer.

"I don't know what is to come and I can't make a promise I may or may not be able to keep. After all this is war, we are going off to. Many of us will die, that's the scary truth of this all.  But I will fight like bloody hell to stay alive and make it back to you Saoirse, so we can grow old together and you can spend the rest of your days reminding me to pick up my clothes off the floor." Aiden chuckled as he kissed me softly.  Rolling my eyes with a faint smile on my face,

"I love you Aiden Palo," I said, then he kissed me one last time, holding back my tears "I love you my darling Saoirse," Aiden yelled back as he was walking towards Jimmy, Calloway and Henry.

"I love you to Aiden!" I yelled, waving back one last time before

Abby and I started to make our way back home. Our hearts aching with fear and dread. Soon as we made our way inside, we both collapsed on the floor holding on to one another. Our tears falling from our faces, and for the first time ever in our lives, we both had not a clue of what our futures would become.

# Chapter Nine
## Aiden and Jimmy

Bootcamp was one of the hardest things I had ever endured. I would come to rethink later, but for as in this moment this was it took the cake. All the countless drills we had to run, the constant berating and condescending yelling tactics, would push me to my limits every day, but I refused to give up. Jimmy, Callaway, Henry and I all had enlisted one month ago from today. Jimmy and I were enlisted in the British Army, and Callaway and Henry were enlisted in the Royal British Air Force.

That there is the difference between those of us who had college degrees and those of us who did not. But I didn't mind it, I knew once we arrived, I would be suited better here. I knew I could excel here. The first day of bootcamp we were assigned to the 21$^{st}$ army group. We were made up of British, Canadian, Dutch, American, Czech soldiers, among several others. Our Drill Sergeant, Sergeant William 'The Bull' Nance was someone I despised of in the beginning, but in time, would grow and admire him in the end. He had previously served in World War 1 and had garnished his nickname 'The Bull' due to his unwavering strategic attacks against the enemy at that time. Like a bull he would charge into battle without hesitation. He was a decorated sergeant, well on his way to captain and Major no doubt about that. He was firm but fair and I had respected that about him. We spent two months in bootcamp. Training and learning various field exercise drills, how to clean and use our weapons. All Basic military tactics and maneuvers. Then after that, for the next 6 months we would perform several military operations in various locations throughout England. Jimmy and I had managed to stay in the same group which gave us both a sense of comfort and ableness to push one another as much as we needed to at times.

Every day I thought about Saoirse, I thought about home. I prayed hard, that she would be kept safe out of harm's way. I wrote her every day giving her insight of my day-to-day routines and how much I missed her. I had just sat down on my cot to begin writing Saoirse another letter when our sergeant walked in, "ATTENTION!" Private Dowell yelled out.

We all got up, standing in a perfect line formation, feet together hands straight at out sides. Saluting our sergeant when he walked in. "Men at ease," Nance said, "we have just received word and here are our first set of orders. We will be shipping out tomorrow at 0600 hours into France. Our briefing on this mission will be in the East Hall at 0400 hours tonight. You boys got that?" Sergeant Nance asked.

"Sir, yes Sir!" we all saluted as we responded in unison, then sergeant Nance turned around and left the left the room.

I looked over at Jimmy who was grinning from ear to ear, our time has finally come. All the hours spent training, drills after drills and now, we are finally going to have boots on the ground.

"Finally, we will get to see some of our own action here boys," Jimmy exclaimed, "Except you Nikolai they told me that you were benched do to not meeting the height requirement for the jump," Jimmy laughed as Nikolai punched him in the arm. The playful banter continued as we made our way to the briefing that evening.

'Alright men, we will be sending you all into France. Your whereabouts will be given here by your Platoon Officer. I have absolute faith and confidence in you men to complete the task that will be given at hand. Good luck and Godspeed," Major Briggs said.

Once he had left the stage, Sergeant Nance, along with First Lieutenant Davis both going over the course of action and what to expect as the briefing ended. They ordered us all to get our affairs in order as we left the building. That night I headed back to my bed and began writing out my letter I had previously started to Saoirse, and one to my parents. Once I was done with them both, I stuck them in a sealed plastic bag for safe keeping. I walked over to the affairs office, the young lady at the front desk had confirmed all my information was correct in case of my untimely death, everything would be left to Saoirse.

I lied in bed that night more anxious than I have ever been, but also slightly eager to get out there and provide support to our brothers on the frontlines. After all, "This is exactly what we have been prepared for," I thought to myself as I shut my eyes and went to sleep.

# Chapter Ten
## Callaway and Henry

Aiden and Jimmy had been placed in the British Royal Army, as for Henry and I we were able to enlist into the British royal air force. Our college degrees had given us both the starting ranks of First Lieutenant. The thought of leaving home and going to war made my heart heavy. The possibility of being separated from Henry during battle was something I try constantly to suppress my thoughts from venturing to.

Bootcamp was Hell, as I expected it to be, but once it was over I was extremely eager to continue my education, and soon to be completing my pilot training. We both would be flying A Supermarine Spitfire. A Fighter aircraft, the spitfire, was designed as a short-range high-performance model. She was beautiful, having an elliptical wing with innovative sunken rivets so I can have the thinnest cross section possible, and was able to achieve the highest of top speeds, greater than that of its other fighter crafts, including the Hawker Hurricane. She had me in a chokehold and I couldn't wait to get in the cockpit. Our class courses flew by like a breeze and just in a few short weeks we were ready to take our first flights to the sky.

The morning dew sat on the plane's wings as I skimmed my fingers gently over the metal framing, collecting the water on my fingertips. Henry was just across the way from my plane, doing the same as I, and admiring his own plane.

"She's a thing of beauty, isn't she?" Henry yelled over to me. Smiling, I turned back and said, "She sure is..." turning back to admire once more just how perfect this plane truly was. I climbed the ladder and made my way into the cockpit. Checking over the electrics and reviewing our take-off check list. When all clear was given to my ground crew, the cockpit door was shut, and we were in the clear for taxing the runway. I started my plane, the sound of the loud engine roaring underneath me was music to my ears, as we made our way taxing down the runway. When it was my turn for take-off, the tower gave me the 'all go', I pushed my throttle forward picking up speed as I moved further down the runway. When I had reached the proper speed for lift off, I started to pull my joystick towards me allowing for the Spitfire to be lifted off the ground, and for the first time, I felt a surge of excitement and freedom as the earth below me grew smaller the higher I climbed. Over the next several weeks Henry and I trained relentlessly. Flight after flight learning all that we could about our aircraft. Remembering every sound, retaining every fluid motion putting it all to memory, becoming one, man and machine.

We trained like our lives depended on it, because it did. Our first mission was going to be here sooner than we could have ever anticipated. Our final days of flight school were coming to an end. The war was progressing at a rapid rate, and on our final training day, we took one last evening flight. The sunset was beginning to set as we all took to the sky on final time as trainees. Soaring higher and higher watching the ground disappear as I have done time and time before, my mind, up here was always at peace. Up here in the sky, everything seemed to just disappear, all our problems and worries just gone, just me, my flight crew beside me and my plane.

Our squadron was made up of a group of 15 pilot fighters. Henry was to the left of me, as we glided through the sky, the sun slowly disappeared behind the Horizon, the sky turning from various shades of pinks and yellows and orange to a light blue, becoming a darker shade of blue as the sky went from dusk to darkness. We began our descent, making our way towards the tarmac. After I had touched down removed myself from the cockpit, I looked across the field and there stood my whole squadron. Proud of this feeling, I Gathered the boys around and took a group photo. The first and last photograph of my squadron and I, all together alive and well.

# Chapter Eleven
Abby

*November 13th,1938*

*Dear Jimmy,*

*It's been several long months since we both last saw each other. I have longed to hear your voice and feel your touch. I miss those beautiful blue eyes staring back at me. My heart fears for you, as everyday this war grows bigger and more dangerous, I can't help but fear for what's to come. The city is running rampant. We have been in constant disarray, the mass casualties coming in from all over London. They have split the hospitals up into Twelve separate sectors. London being split into six major sectors for mass causalities, then six more makeshift hospital tents have gone up around the countryside.*

*I feel like I have lost more than I have been able to save. That thought weighs heavy on my heart, but don't you go worrying about me my darling, Saoirse and I are doing just fine. I keep looking at my ring, a beautiful reminder that once this war is over with, you will soon make me Mrs. Abby Ruize. I pray for you every night Jimmy, for your safe return, and for the others safe return home as well. I love you for eternity Jimmy. Until we see one another again, stay safe my darling.*

*Eternally yours,*
*Abby*

I folded the letter and placed it in the envelope sealing it with a kiss as I licked the glue and sealed it closed. I placed it in the box along with a few chocolates and some of Jimmy's other favorite snacks and taped it shut. It takes everything in me these days to stay sane and hold my composer. I can't be too honest with him about what's going on, as I need to stay strong and make sure his mental state is healthy for battle. I know he worries enough as is. I write him every day, and God knows how much I miss him. I put on my shoes and coat and proceed to lift the package off the floor and walk out the door and head for the post office.

Saoirse is working the night shift again; I will be joining her in just a few short hours. The seasons are beginning to change here. The air has a slight chill to it as I made my way down towards the post office. Typically, it takes a few weeks to get this package where it's needed, sometimes longer, just depends on the route the cargo planes are forced to take. I noticed all the Christmas decorations as I walked through downtown; in all the chaos, I have forgotten that Christmas is just around the corner. I can't help to think that last year was the last normal year we all had in celebrating any holiday's together.

I finally made it to the post office, quite a few people in here in front of me. I wait patiently for my turn to come. A few moments later I make it to the front desk.

"How can I help you dear?" The sweet old post lady asked me.

"Hello, I need to send this package to the address listed here please," I replied.

"TO: Jimmy Ruize, 21$^{st}$ Army Corp, Surrey, England RH5," The post lady confirmed back to me. "Yes, thank you," I replied.

She then took the box and handed it to the young gentleman behind her, "Will that be all dear?" She asked.

"Yes, thank you," I replied. I turned to leave, before I made it to the door, I heard a loud BOOM! BOOM! BOOM! My body immediately stands still, a shiver makes it way up my spine, I look through the glass of the door up to the sky, that's when I see German Bombers heading towards the city. Dropping bomb after bomb, I quickly run towards the front desk and tell everyone inside to take cover behind the counter. Ducking under the service desk, the old lady who had helped me begins the praying to keep us safe and protect our souls. The fear spread across everyone's faces as we sit silently waiting for this moment to pass.

I cover my ears and close my eyes; I can hear the loud roar of their engines as they make their way towards the city. The bombs continue to drop. BOOM! BOOM! BOOM! Again, and again. What seemed like eternity was only that of a few short moments. When it was done, I opened my eyes and looked around. The post office remained untouched this time I thought, as I crawled out from under the service desk and peeked my head up over the counter, I walked over to the door and wedged it open. Debris from the buildings nearby was blocking the door. Using as much force as I could I pushed it open just about halfway, just enough for us all to slide out through.

The devastation outside was unimaginable. Quickly, I gather my bag and turn to look at everyone behind me. Scanning the room one last time making sure everyone was okay before I stepped outside. The loud screams and cries heard all around me echoing from the collapsed ruble, I didn't know where to begin. Panic was beginning to set in, my hands grew shaky, my palms were sweaty. I told myself to stop and took a deep breath in "You got this; you can do this. Breath in and breath out, take a moment to look around, assess who is in critical need and tend to them first, then move on to the next one, taking it one at a time, you can do this Abby," I said to myself. Quickly coming to my sense, I see a group of people in front me and I start asking them questions. Are you okay? How bad are you injured? Are there any more with you? I give some orders of those around me that can help and begin searching the ruble. I heard the sirens blare in the distance as medics are making their way here.

Just then, something caught the corner of my eye. One man who was covered in blood all over his body, I made my way closer to him and I see his clothes-soaked in dark red blood that covered entire his shirt. I ran over to him asking him where he was hurt. He was in shock, make him sit on a pile of bricks. He had several head wounds that I could see, deep gashes around the back side of his head towards the front of his face. I tear off a piece of cloth from my shirt and begin wrapping it around his head.

"Sir, I'm going to need you to stay awake," I said, I asked him what his name was.

"Sir, what's your name?" he doesn't answer, his face pale white, covered in blood. I make myself eye level with him and I ask again, "sir, I need you to tell me your name," I asked. Again, no response. He is mumbling something, but I can't quite make it out.

Suddenly, he made eye contact with me, wide eyed his breathing pauses, I go to ask him for his name once more, then suddenly he lets out a scream, a blood curdling wail. "I HAD THEM IN MY ARMS, I HAD THEM IN MY ARMS AND NOW I CAN'T FIND THEM!" "WHERE DID THEY GO!?" "I CAN'T FIND THEM!" he shouts repeatedly.

I try to calm him down, but it's of no use, I have no doubts he has lost his family, I took a hold of his hand and tell him I will go look for "them". I said calmly. I made my way down through some ruble piles turning to him, I ask, "what building did you come from?"

He turns to me and his screams come to a dead stop, eyes wide and pale as a ghost he points to the building just to the right of me. Felling a sense of dread and heartache rushing over me, I knew just as well as he did, that his family was gone.

The building destroyed. No one could have survived; it was a miracle he had made it out with his life. Crushed glass and broken bricks from the building laid out all over the ground. I turned to the man, "Can you tell me how many of you were living together? And what their names are?" I ask, feeling like I needed to still try and call out for them.

He looks up at me, tears filling his eyes, and calmly said, "there is no use, they are all dead," he replied.

He puts his hands to his face and started to sob. Even though I knew that was true I couldn't help but at least go over there and try. I removed brick after brick, my bare hands bleeding from glass and other debris pieces.

I yelled out "IS ANYONE ALIVE?" "CAN YOU HEAR ME?" IS ANYONE THERE?" I wait, I am silent for a few seconds, hoping I can hear anything. Yelling, screaming, banging, just give me anything at all to let me know someone is alive, but all I get is silence in return.

I pause to look around me, people running, carrying their loved ones in their arms. Some dead, others missing limbs, salty tears fill my eyes and fall from my face, my hands covered in blood. I resend down from the collapsed building as the noises around me start to rush back and fill my ears again. I see the ambulances in the distance trying to make their way through the scattered debris in the road. I run over to meet them; they swing open their doors, one medic jumps out of the ambulance while the other hands him his medic bag, they both start to unload the gurney.

"Hello, my name is Abby, I am a nurse at St Giles Hospital," I said as I approached the first medic.

"We have at least ten people who are in critical need to get to the hospital first. The others can wait for the rest of the ambulances to arrive," I said to medic number one.

He pauses for a moment and then looks at me, "I'm sorry miss but no other ambulances are coming." Medic, one said.

Puzzled I stammered as I started to respond.

"Wai…wait what do you mean there are no other ambulances coming?" I asked.

"There are too many areas in need of assistance, and we have been stripped thin." Medic, one said to me.

"We need to get these people to the hospital, or they will die! We need more ambulances." I shouted at him.

Medic one turned to me. "Miss, I am aware of the desperate help these people are in, but we are doing our best with what we have. I can try and take as many as I can, but that is all I can do, okay?! So please stop yelling at me and let me do my job," Medic one said.

I took a minute and processed what he was saying, and he was right. There was nothing that we could do other than save as many as we can right now.

"Okay, I am sorry it's just been a tense several minutes," I said back to him.

"I know, now can you help me get the most critical ones that are able to be saved into the ambulance?" Medic, one asked.

"Yes, of course," I replied.

We both begin to put those in need of critical care in the ambulances first, we had at least 4 of them loaded, when a man in his truck and a few others behind him pulled up.

"How can we be of assistance?" The man asked stepping out of his truck.

I waved him over, "Can you take the rest of the critically injured people in your truck?" I asked the gentleman.

"Of course, we can fit as many as we can in the back of the cab and in the bed of the truck," he tells me.

"Okay, and the rest of those that are not critical we will divide amongst the other trucks," I said back to the gentleman.

Nodding in agreement, we were all on the same page as we moved person after person into the back of each truck. After everyone was loaded on up, I hopped into the ambulance and rode with the paramedics to the hospital. My hands started to tremble again; I shake them trying to make them steady.

"It's the adrenaline," I said to myself trying to do breathing techniques to calm my nerves.

We soon arrive at the hospital, which is still standing thank God, for a moment I had forgotten about Saoirse and the other hospital staff. I guess I had assumed it to be in good standing because the other possibility was unfathomable to think about at the time. I stepped out of the ambulance quickly to help the patients out. One by one the hospital staff rush out to help. I took a moment and look up, there stood Saoirse at the hospital doors, that moment, with all the chaos around me, I found comfort in her face and just then my hands stop shaking and I made my way into the hospital.

# Chapter Twelve
## Saoirse

These days seem to be everlasting, one day merges into the next and suddenly it's a new week and new month. I try and focus on the positive things we have such as our life, while so many others have perished. My parents worry about me constantly, they want me to come home and be with them. It's hard for them to have me here, but they also understand this is where I am needed. I phone as much as I can to check in and see how they are doing. Aiden has been in my dreams every night since he has left. I find comfort and solace there, in his smile and those beautiful green eyes staring back into mine. The way he intertwines my fingers in his and pulled me in close. He could calm my nerves with just one simple touch. His presence, I crave infinitely. I retreat to my quiet office to begin writing my letter to him.

*December 13th, 1938*

*Dear Aiden,*

*I find comfort in my dreams with you. These days, comfort and happiness seem to be in short supply. I'm so proud of you, my love. The days here can be long and burdensome. The sun is out, but there is no happiness, no joy. I have been working tirelessly at the hospital, my days have begun to blur together.*

*I have forgotten Christmas is just around the corner. The hospital staff has put up a few decorations to help bring back some joy that has been lost. I talked to your parents just the other day, they seem to be doing as good as one can be doing in these circumstances.*

*I had a wonderful dream about us the other night, we were at my parents' house, and the backyard was full of wildflowers, it was the beginning of summer. The smell of my mum's peach pie was aromatic, I swear I could taste it in mouth as I slept. I could hear my mum laughing in the background from a joke my dad had made.*

*I look out into the field, and I see you. Your dark brown skin, shinning as the sunlight danced over your body. Your attention was on something, just there, standing before you. I followed your gaze and there in the flowers stood a small child. I couldn't make out if the child was a boy or girl, as there back was turned to me, their hair was dark brown, with loose curls that just hugged the back of their neck.*

*The laughing and sounds of giggles echoed through the air, you had your arms out as our little one made their way into them. You swopped our baby up and began twirling around holding on tightly. I look on at you both, admiring the beauty of the moment. I close my eyes as I listen to the sounds the birds are making all around me. I look back at you once more holding our little one, you both start to turn around and walk towards me, I try to make out our babies face, but before all the features could be made clear, I was awoken.*

*I think about that dream often, and what our future life will hold for us... Just know that I and Abby are both safe. I'll keep you in my dreams as I know you will keep me in yours. Before we know it, we will soon be holding onto one another again, never to let each other go. I love you my sweet darling Aiden.*

*Your beloved,*
*Saoirse*

I fold the letter up and shove it in my pocket for it will be safe there for now until I can mail it off tomorrow. I try to lay down to catch some much-needed rest. I close my eyes, but just then a massive BOOM! Sound that goes off. My heart sinks into my stomach.

Bombs, they are dropping bombs on the city. I quickly reach the door and run out into the hospital hallway. Gathering all the I can patients and tucking them under desks, in closets, anywhere we can take cover from the bombings.

The hospital shakes as the bombs continue dropping. Getting louder as they move closer, I close my eyes and hold my breath, they are now within a few buildings from ours. I clinch my teeth as the next bomb goes off, on after another. One bomb hitting closely to the hospital, rattling it, causing some of the windows to shatter. I open my eyes and say Abby's name under my breathe, in that moment it had occurred to me she was on her way to the post office not too far from here.

Fear overcomes my body as I think about her and her safety.

"Oh god" I think to myself.

"Please, please don't be there," I said to myself.

"Maybe she went earlier in the day," I said again,

"God, Abby you better not be there." I close my eyes once more sending out a prayer for us all and for Abby. Silence suddenly fills the air for a few moments more. Then the cries soon echoed out, as we move to get the patients back into their perspective bedrooms and assess any damage nearby.

The hospital had a few shattered windows, glass all over the floor, could have been worse, much worse. But for now, it was safe at least for this time around. Once all the patients were settled back in, we gathered more medical supplies dispersing it all around, tucking bandages, morphine, suture kits, etc... putting them all within arm's reach. We knew there was going to be mass causalities flooding the hospital doors soon. We moved the least critical patients out of the lower-level rooms and up on the 2$^{nd}$ and 3$^{rd}$ floors. I was gathering supplies, when I heard over our radio, "WE HAVE MULTPILE VICTIMS COMING IN, I REPEAT ALL HOSPTAL STAFF BE OUT FRONT AND READY TO RECEIVE PATIENTS!" the medic repeated over the radio. I finish collecting more supplies and trays, I walk out of the supply room saying under my breath,

"Abby you better be home." I said to myself.

About an hour went by, we could hear the sirens in the distance getting louder as they approached the hospital. All of us ready and eager to help as the ambulance made its way through the streets. "Okay, everyone, most critical victims first, make sure to label in their charts the morphine dosages, we do not want to have any accidental over dosages. Most importantly, remember to stay calm, there will be a lot of screaming, crying, and panic from the patients. It is our job not to try and keep them calm. I know you all have what it takes to do this, it's what we have been trained for. Work as a team, and we will be fine," I said.

Just then, the ambulance made its approach. The vehicles doors swung open upon its immediate stoppage.

A young man jumps out and started to unload the victims. One at a time, each victim was brought in. The nurses were checking their vitals and making their wound assessments, working alongside the doctors in one fluid motion. I scanned each victims face looking for Abby's, praying she was not one of the victims here. As the final victim was being unloaded from the ambulance I, for a split moment, looked over and there she was. Abby was coming out of the ambulance helping unload the last victim. In a quick second I make eye contact with her, giving her a nod and a mere smile, as the rush of relief washings over me knowing she, indeed is alive. She gives me a faint smile back, while making her way into the hospital, both getting to work.

The bodies kept flowing in, one after another. Children, women, and men of all ages. Some had their Limbs missing, others had their bones broken, several had their bones protruding through their skin. Those with second- and third-degree burns covering their entire body, screaming in pain at the top of their lungs. It was unlike anything. I had ever seen before. Their screams, my god their screams seemed to be never ending. My heart ached for them, we administrated each burn victim with the maximum dose of morphine in hopes to help ease their pain, but for some, the burns were so bad that even with the max morphine dosage their pain was unbearable.

In the hallway I see one victim whose head had been severely lacerated; she was bleeding profusely. I gently lay her down on the gurney, taking her vitals, the blood from her head was dripping onto the floor, covering parts of my shoes. My nurses gown, drenched in bright red blood.

I grabbed some medical supplies and began to attend to her wounds, but when I turned around, she was still, her chest wasn't moving up and down. I could not hear her labored breathing anymore. I walked over to her, lying there on the bed, her arm was cold to the touch, I knew she was gone. I placed her hands together on her stomach and placed a sheet over her body. I said a silent prayer for her soul, then quickly moved onto the next patient.

Patient after patient loss after loss it seemed like a never-ending cycle of death all around me. For several hours, this went on, feeling as if this was never going to cease, until it did.  Finally, a break in the chaos. I get myself cleaned up and made my way down the hall, to find Abby. Through all the chaos we both become separated. I see her at the front desk and made my way over to her. She was sitting in a chair off to the side of the counter, no doubt lost in her thoughts, trying to process the events of today.

I gently touch her shoulder, snapping her back from wherever her mind had taken her.

"Are you okay?" I asked Abby.

Giving me a slight smile, she took a deep breath and lets it out, "I'm alive," she said to me with tears in her eyes.

I took her hand in mine, "Let's go home," I said to her, we both get up to go grab our things. Upon returning from my office, we say goodnight to all the other women. Exhausted, and without a doubt starving, we begin to make our way home.

Our walk home was a quiet one, both lost in our own thoughts, too tired to put into words. Today, was one of the worst days since the war had begun. And for the foreseeable future, this was our new reality.

# Chapter Thirteen
## The Drop

"We are doing a night drop into Saarland, Germany. 10 divisions dropping all at once. We will be taking on heavy fire from the Germans down below," Sergeant Nance continued. "I'm not going to sugar coat it boys, this will be unlike anything you have seen before, but I know, you are all more than prepared. Make us proud and try to stay alive," Nance finished.

After the briefing, we were all heading back to our barracks, gathering our bags. I was lost in deep thought when jimmy came up from behind me putting me in a head lock.

"You ready to take on some Krauts mate?" he laughs jokingly while ruffling my hair. I push him away and remove my head from his armpit, "I'm as ready as I can be you crazy bastard," I sarcastically said.

"Well as long as we have each other's backs we will destroy anything, especially, any kraut that's headed our way," Jimmy said seemingly.

"To be honest, I'm not so sure how I feel, but I'll tell you one thing Jimmy," I said to him.

"what's that?" Jimmy said.

"Let's promise each other, no hero shit, alright mate? We both need to make it back home to our beautiful loves," I said.

With a big ole smile, putting his hand to his head in a salute formation, "Roger, Roger their peter rabbit," Jimmy joked.

Laughing, I smacked his hand from his face, "sarcastic cunt," I said to him. Once we made it to our barracks, we both gathered our bags, double checking we have all we needed in our packs. We would be heading out early in the morning, the sky will be still dark, just before dawn would be approaching.

At 0300 hours we made our way to the tarmac. The plane's engines roared heavy and loud, you could barely hear others speak, let alone your own thoughts. We all loaded onto the planes and took off into the dead of night. We climbed higher and higher up into the clouds above. It would be at least a couple of hours before we hit the drop zone.

They gave us all anti nauseous pills, one for before take-off and the other for mid-flight. Nerves were racing through some of the men, fiddling with their weapons or messing with their packs. While some others seemed unfazed and took this opportunity to nap. As for me, I usually am calm by nature when it comes to intense situations. Jimmy was sitting across from me; he too is one that is unfazed by what's to come.

Jimmy decided to get some sleep as we flew into the night. I close my eyes, trying to get some sleep as well. You never know when sleep will come next. I begin to doze off, was only for a few short moments when suddenly, our plane started taking on heavy fire. Bombs going off, bullets coming at us from down below. The red signal popped on, signaling us that it's time to hook up. Once that light turns green, we are good to jump.

Planes around us were also taking on heavy fire, blowing up before the soldiers were able to make their jump. Whole squads, up in flames in an instant. I gave my men the signal and started the check off, go for twelve, go for eleven, go for ten, go for nine, go for eight, go for seven, go for six, go for five, go for four, go for three, go for two and I being first in line, all go for one. Our plane taking several more hits, hitting the left engine. We started to rapidly descend. I signaled our men to jump as the light turned green. One by one we all jumped into the air shoots out trying to avoid all firing from down below. From up above, the sky looked like it was filled with millions of fireflies, but it just the Muzzle Flash.

Debris was falling everywhere. Men jumping from planes with unopened shoots, others were on fire, and many had been hit by gun fire on the way down. I landed, hard on my side, and immediately pulled my shoot off me and grabbed my gun attached to my pack. I searched for others in my squadron, moving quickly and quietly keeping low to the ground, Germans were laying down firing all around me.

I find O'Reilly and Flannagan immediately, both landed near me. I tell them to keep low and keep quiet.

"Do either of you have your weapons?" I asked them.

"No, we both had lost ours in the jump," Flannagan said.

"Okay, use your knife from your packs or your pistol if you have it. Stay low and follow me. If you find a weapon, pick it up. Got it?" I said.

"Yes, sir," they both replied.

We continued to move forward looking for more soldiers. I couldn't find Jimmy anywhere, after O'Reilly and Flannagan, I had found Squires, 'Frenchie' Frank, Nikolai, Miles and Duke. But no sign of Jimmy, my stomach was beginning to turn and feel anxious at the thought something could have happened to Jimmy on the way down.

We continued to move on forward gathering a few more men, Wallace, Williams and Jackson. None of which were part of my squad. They were from division 2 squadron.

"Has anyone seen Sergeant Nance?" I asked the men

"Lieutenant Briggs?" I asked. Neither of which had been seen since before the jump.

"Okay, let's continue eastward to our target area, any one left will head in the same direction. Meet up and gather our bearings at the ronde Vue point Got it?" I said to the men. They all shook their heads in agreeance.

Moving eastward, we walked for only a few miles when out of the trees ahead I see Jimmy.

"Jimmy!" I whispered. Stopping in his tracks, he turns towards the direction he heard his name. I move into the moonlight, lighting my face so he could see who was calling him. Walking towards him, once I reached Jimmy, I patted him on his shoulder, "Man it's good to see you. I thought you had gotten lost out here since your navigation skills are shite an all without me" I said to him.

He slaps my hand away, "Rubbish, mate you couldn't lose me I'm attached to you like a bloody cockroach," Jimmy said jokingly.

"I'm glad I found ya mate," I replied. "Okay there is seven of us from our squad. We picked up 3 more from division 2 squad William, Wallace and Jackson," I explained.

"Hey" they said in unison.

"Howdy, gents," Jimmy replied

"Okay, that's all for introductions for now let's do a weapons count and ammo check," I asked.

"Jimmy, Duke, O'Reilly empty your bags and let's see what we got," I ordered.

Dumping all their ammo in a pile, "It looks like we have 5 rifles, and 200 rounds of ammo. A couple knives and 10 frags," I counted out.

I took the map out and proceeded to mark how far we had to walk to our ronde Vue point.

"Alright, looks like we head east for about 4 clicks then we should be at our ronde Vue point in Saarlean," I informed the men.

"Eyes sharp boys, stay quiet and don't make any sudden movements. We are still in enemy territory boys," I affirmed to the group.

Making our way eastward, we walked all night into the early morning hours. Hungry, and sleep deprived we continued for about 2 more clicks when we came upon our base camp. I ordered my men to grab water, food and rest for the time being while I go and get some answers. See if anyone has heard from Lieutenant Briggs or Sergeant Nance. I walked over to the captains tent, lone and behold sergeant Nance was standing there before me. I stood immediately at attention saluting him.

"At ease private," he continued, "I heard you were quite the leader out there today. Taking charge when needed. Damn proud of you son," Nance said.

"Thank you, sir, I have you to thank for that," I said.

"Sir? Have you heard from Lieutenant Briggs? We got separated after the drop and I haven't seen him since. Everyone I have asked has not seen or heard from him either," I stated.

Sergeant Nance dropped his head slightly, "We lost a lot of good men out there. A lot have been scattered about to God knows where. Lieutenant Briggs has not made contact since the drop, and you are all that is left of your division. So, for the time being, I will be promoting you from private to lieutenant. Your act of bravery and take-charge leadership attitude is what we need," Sergeant Nance said. "Wow, thank you sir, I don't know what to say," I said.

Stunned and shocked, Nance shook my hand and saluting him as I left to head back to my men and.

Lieutenant Palo, I kind of like the sound of that I thought to myself.

# Chapter Fourteen
## The Flight

Our first mission was approaching rapidly. Many of the other crews we have watched leaving, going out in Flanks of 15 only to have 4 or 5 return. Many, of whom were friends of ours. Henry and I, put our family affairs in order and wrote our perspective letters.

The day before our strike we had a briefing in the hanger.

"You men will be heading out at 1200 hours. Your mission is to take out all the land locked guns, and as many tanks as you can so our teams down below can move in on their ground invasion. Our ground forces have been pushed back and are holding the ranks in Saarlean," Major Ruger continued, "once you have hit your selected targets, return home steadfast. Get in and get out. We have lost too many men, so be vigilant and stay sharp. I have faith in you all, good luck and God bless," Major Ruger finished.

After Major Ruger left, first lieutenant Stevens and second Lieutenant Mitchell went into further description of our mission plan. After the briefings we all went to the mess hall and had ourselves what they call "the last supper" serving up the best dish the royal air force has to offer before our send off. After supper, we had a few hours to kill. I encouraged my crew to grab a some shut eye before we head out for the night.

1200 hours came upon us fast. My crew standing at attention in front of me. Over the course of training, I had been promoted from 1<sup>st</sup> lieutenant to Captain, finally a crew of my own.

"Now boys, this is what we have been training for, I'm not going to bullshit you, out there, it will be like nothing you have experienced before. But I have absolute faith, that every one of you will hit your targets and make it back home safely. After all, we are the best damn flight crew there ever is," I said to my men, "You all heard Major Ruger, stay sharp, get in and get out, and no heroics! You hear me? I don't want to have to mail back any of your belongings to your families alright?!" I finished.

"YES SIR" my men replied.

We all broke off and made our way to our planes. My crew was made up of 12 pilots split into 2 flight crews. Then, they Added an additional flight crew, Squadron 6, made up of 10 pilots. 22 planes in all, made up of strikers and bombers. We started our engines; the roaring sounds and the engines vibrations always give me a sense of ease. I finished my final flight check and took to the runway. The others followed, 2-3 at a time taking off from the airstrip. The sky filling with bombers and fighter planes. I'm sure it was as a beautiful scene from down below, I had imagined.

Our flight would take about an hour in a half to reach our destination. The clouds up above hid the lights of the cities down below. We, by now were over halfway into our flight. I knew we would be approaching our target zone soon. Over the radio, I spoke, "Okay boys, we are about to approach our target zone. There will be heavy fire from down below once we clear these clouds. Remember hit your marks and get out. I want to see every last one of you back home. Alright boys, get ready, here go, God speed to you all," I finished on the coms.

Henry's plane was to the left of me. I looked over and I could see him smiling and giving his nod of appreciation. The clouds began to dissipate in front of us. Just a matter of moments before they would disappear, and our cover was gone. We began our descent on down through the clouds and once cleared, we took on Immense fire as we dove down out of the clouds. I gripped the controls with ferocity firing my guns trying to hit as many of my targets as I could. The roar of the gun fire filled my ears. Henrys plane had taking lead, the sky filling with enemy fighter jets just as we circled back around for a second go of it.

Clearing a path for the bombers to make their drops, we broke off flanking left and right hitting as many enemy planes as we could. Pushing my aircraft to its limits, banking right and left, dodging incoming fire from the ground and all around me. Just before I was about to take out another gunner, an enemy plane flanked me from behind. I banked hard to the left then to the right, trying to shake him from my tail, he was one hell of a pilot, but I knew, I was better. I went straight up into the sky, a barrel spin as I climbed higher, when I reached the right velocity and height, I pulled back on my lever dipping my plane above him, positioning myself behind him. In that moment, I locked on to him and fired at will. His plane was hit several times. Several of my bullets catching him in the engines which caught his plane on fire, and he began to spiral down towards the ground, exploding into flames when his plane hit the ground. A moment later another plane came up to my right wing, out maneuvering him I was able to hit his plane several times taking him out as well. Two more planes came in from behind me, I was able to shake one of them, but the second had popped off a few rounds hitting my right-wing engine. He locked onto my plane for the second time, going in for the kill shot. At this point, my electronics where failing.

Here, in what I thought would be my final moments. He locked on to me and just as he was about to fire, Air fire had come from behind the enemy plane, he was hit and going down. I looked around scanning side to side, when there I saw Henry's plane. He had gotten to me just in time, giving him a thumbs up signal of "I'm okay" I was able to get my plane steady and under control. Our targets were cleared, our mission was completed, and we were all making our way back to base.

Upon arriving back at base, I took roll call. We had lost 12 planes, 6 of those were bomber planes. 12 pilots, 10 copilots. The 6 bomber planes had crew teams of 8 in each plane. 70 men in total lost their lives today. 70 great men, no not men, but boys, 70 boys were dead. I lost 5 pilots from my own crew alone. This ache in my heart was heavy. Survivors guilt was an unfamiliar feeling until now. Having made it out alive, while the others were less fortunate, a feeling I would come to know all too well in the end.

Back in our barracks, I dropped my pack off after our debriefing. "What's going on in that head of yours?" Henry asked.
So much was running through my brain, the mission, and what I could have done differently. Our friends, Charlie, Tyler, Devon, Max and Samuel. Friends I had hoped to have for lifetime, were just gone in an instant. It was naive thinking on my part, especially during war. They won't be the last friends I will lose either. As my thoughts started to sink deeper into a depressive state, I responded before Henry would notice something was wrong.
 "Nothing, just glad we made it home safely," I said with a half-smile, "I think I'm going to get some shut eye though," I said.
Henry squeezed my shoulder gently, "you can't save them all Calloway, we are going to lose some and save some. Don't hold on to those we have lost, otherwise it will tear you apart," Henry said.
He then got up, "I'm going to the mess hall, if you change your mind I'll be there," Henry said.
Smiling back at him I squeezed his hand. When he left, I rolled to my

side; fading in and out of sleep, until I would finally succumbed to the exhaustion and closed my eyes to get some sleep.

54

# Chapter Fifteen
### Saoirse

It's been 3 long years since the war began. My city, London had air raids for 57 nights In September of 1940. We had constant bombs that were being dropped on our city. Buildings collapsed, homes destroyed, our hospital was partially bombed almost a year ago. We had managed to come out unscathed until they carpet bombed the eastern part of the city in the middle of the night, taking out half the hospital and many of my collogues and friends. Many patients perished that dreadful night. I could hear the bombers coming. I shot out of bed at the sound of their planes flying over our building. When I ran to my window I could see the flashing light from the explosion. Vibrating the entire building.

I looked out the window once more and saw a few planes moving towards the hospital. They were going to target the hospitals, all over the city. I got dressed and quickly ran to grab Abby, she too was already dressed. We grabbed our bags and ran out the door. When we arrived at the hospital it was up in flames. I could hear patients screaming making their way out of the hospital. I was looking for our Head Chief, scanning the crowd for his face but I was unable to find him anywhere. Abby and I were grabbing as many people as we could pull out from the first floor. Smoke bellowed everywhere making it incredibly hard to breathe, my eyes were watering and stung from all the smoke.

The fire rescue had arrived and started to put out the fires. Once the flames were out and the smoke had settled, we had assessed the damage that was done. They took out the west wing of the hospital, which was filled with our elder patients. We had managed to get most of the people out and into the street while we waited for help to arrive. We had only a few patients who sadly, had perished in the fire, no children were harmed thank God for that. We lost 6 colleagues and our Head Chief Doctor.

Chief Doctor John D. Lewis was the last one to leave. Making sure all his patients and staff were out before he was going to leave.

While helping to remove the babies and children, he had gone back to look once more for anyone else and that's when another plane had flown over and dropped a second bomb. The explosion engulfing the west wing even more, going up in flames and taking him and 6 others with it. Upon his passing, I was made head Chief Doctor that day, I was the only one who was more than qualified to take on the responsibilities of my predecessor. That there, was over a year ago almost to the day. Fast forward to present day, December of 1942, London was beginning to rebuild itself as the air raids became less frequent, as the war raged on.

December here, the air is cold, frozen, my brittle bones shake uncontrollably as I stand in line to get some bread and cheese for Abby and I. Food has become relatively scarce. Bread, milk and cheese seem to be the only thing being sent in from other countries as aid. Chocolate is one of the few rare food items we get dropped in with the shipments from time to time. Abby and I had started a garden before the war had begun. A small one on our balcony, growing basil, thyme and peppermint. We would make the drive to the countryside and visit my parents who would supply us with carrots, potatoes and chicken from their farm, as well as any other fruits and vegetables within season.

Standing at the corner of the market waiting for my turn to gather what we needed bread, milk and cheese for the week a cold wind blew in causing my face to remain frozen in its position.

"Snow is on the horizon," I thought to myself. I made my way on home and think of Aiden as I walk along the ponds edge where he had proposed. The pond was calm and very still, I could see my breaths with every exhale I took. I smile at the memory of that wonderful day, living rent free in my head. How quickly everything had gone from being so full of life and security, to fear, panic, and uncertainty. I say a small pray for Aiden and the others, sending it off hoping he hears my words and returns home safely soon enough.

I arrived at home, and put the milk, bread and cheese away I unbutton my coat and put it on the coat rack by the door, then remove my scarf, hat and gloves placing them in their perspective spots. I call out for Abby, "In here!" she said, I follow the corridor down to the back bedroom. She has been knitting us socks and gloves for the winter months to come and has also been knitting some clothing items and blankets for the patients down at the hospital.

I walk into her bedroom and knock faintly on the door.

"Hey Abby," I say leaning against the doorway.

"I was able to get most of the items on our list, plus they had a couple bars of chocolate left, so naturally I grabbed two of those as well," I said to her.

"Oh, well isn't that quite some luck, I could fancy a bit of chocolate myself right about now," she said, giggling.

"Here," she hands me a pile of gloves, sweaters, hats plus much more place them into my arms.

"This pile can be brought to the hospital tonight," she said to me. I scan the room looking for a bag or box to put these in. Abby lets out a cute eek "Look at how cute these mittens are for the babies, all the little booties and hats and sweaters. I even knitted some baby blankets," she said gleefully.

I smile back at her and think to myself how wonderful it is to have a friend like Abby, she finds joy in the littlest of things, I admire her for that. Abby is my Ying to my yang; she always has been and always will be. I hold up some of the items she has knitted grinning,

"These are adorable Abby," I said to her admiring her talent.

"Aren't they though," she said. I nod and smile back at her as I begin to put it all in a box to take to the hospital for our shift tonight.

"Alright all the blankets, mittens, hats, gloves etc... Have all been packed. Are you ready to head out to the hospital? I ask. I want to get there a little early tonight," I said.

"Yes, let me just grab my coat, I made us some sandwiches for dinner as well," Abby replied as she makes her way to the kitchen to grab our dinner out of the fridge. She placed the 2 bags and one box of mixed clothing items on the dining table. We both grab our coats and scarves; I look around trying to remember where I placed my keys at. I started to pat my coat jacket, "where did I put my keys, I could have sworn..." I said puzzled.

"Here they are" Abby said, "you left them on the table by the bag." Stifling a laugh, "I would lose my head if it wasn't for you. Thank you," I replied.

"Well, if that isn't the first honest thing you have ever said I don't know what is!" Abby said laughing.

We both headed out the door and headed towards the hospital. The temperature had dropped rapidly from the time I left the market, to now. "I think it might snow tonight I reckon," I said as I pulled my arms to my body, trying to conserve the heat from escaping.

"Yes, looks to be a beautiful night, let's hope it stays quiet," Abby replied. We both continued as we approached the hospital, the sun had completely set, and dusk was upon us.

The hospital was quiet, we set our bags down and the 2 bags and 1 box full of the knitted items, with plans to disperse them later in the night. We both walked to my office and hung our coats and scarves up. Abby walked out first, making her way to go check on some her patients. I walked to the front desk checking some of the chart sheets, I followed up with the other nurses on their day, patient notes and their end shift details. We had a few new patients admitted, 2 young kids who had lost both parents in a bombing, just south of London.

The older boy looked to be about 8, and his younger sister looked to be 4. Neither one was willing to speak to any of the other nurses. Something I came to understand, it was a common side effect from the trauma they have endured. I walked into their bedroom, I grabbed a chair to sit and be at eye level with both kids.

"Hello, my name is Doctor Saoirse Palo. Can you tell me your name?" I asked the little boy. No response.

"Is it okay if I check your vitals and look at your wounds?" I asked. They both sat there in silence as I started to put new dressings and bandages on both of their wounds. A nice gash on the little boys left arm, it had required stitches, he had a broken right arm that was in a sling, and a minor head wound, but nothing to serious, he was a lucky kid. I turned to his sister next to treat her wounds.

"Hello, how are you doing darling?" I asked the little girl. No response, "is it okay if I look at your wounds and change your bandages like I did you brothers?" I asked her.

The little girl lifted her head, barely making eye contact with me and nodded, yes. She had some minor cuts and bruises, one bad gaping wound on her thigh.

"Whoever fixed these two up did a great job," I said to Becca, one of the other Head Nurses here.

"Okay, I'm all done love, would you two like to have some dinner brought in?" I asked. Still nothing but silence, "If you eat some dinner, I have a chocolate bar you two can split," I said, hoping to entice them to talk or make some kind of gesture. The little girls head shot up, eyes widen, and a smile beamed from her face.

"You both eat your dinner, then afterwards I will come back and give you both a piece of chocolate, but only if you eat your dinner," I said as I stood up from my chair, moving it back against the wall.

I smiled back at the little girl as I made my way to exit the room. Her brother still looking down at the floor, my heart ached for them and the many more who have come before them. Orphaned children who will forever be haunted by the horrors they have seen.

"Okay, I have to go back and attend to my other patients, but I will return with some chocolate later on okay," I affirmed. The little girl shook her head excitedly as I walked out of the room.

An hour passed by, and I had kept to my promise and returned with the chocolate for them both. They devoured it in an instant. Their chocolate covered faces, so precious, for a moment they were just kids again. I left them to Martha; she will tuck them in for the night. I walked through the hospital halls checking on patient after patient, the night was quiet. I had meet up with Abby to take our break and get some food. The sandwiches she had made were plain, but filling, Bread and cheese with a little bit of butter.

We finish up our dinner and head back to work only a few more hours left, and we will head on home to rest for a bit and I, will back here again for the day shift. As I was walking with Abby in the hallway we heard the sound of gun fire outside the building. Abby and I grabbed another and started sprinting to the front of the hospital. We ran down the hallway, through the side door, down 2 flights of stairs to the main floor.

"Where is that coming from?" I asked Becca, who was sitting at the front desk as I catch my breath.

Before anyone could respond another round of gunfire was let off, this time closer to the hospital. I ran to the front doors, looking around scanning the street and sidewalks. I couldn't see anything at first, then that's when I saw them, a group of Nazi Soldiers, at least 6 that I could quickly make out, headed towards us. I yelled back to the others "It's the Nazis!" I shouted.

Panic was beginning to set in amongst the group, I ran back to the desk gathered all the nurses around me, "Okay, listen we need to get all the children and hide them. As many as we can, those who can walk and anyone you need to carry, do so but get as many of them down to the basement hurry," I demanded.

Those soldiers were coming into this hospital, and we need to do what we could to protect everyone.

"Saoirse, if they see we have helped all the soldiers that are in the east wing they will execute them and us. We will be seen as traitors," Abby panicked.

She was right if they catch us with any of these soldiers, they will kill everyone in this hospital.

"I know, okay Abby take Rose, Martha and Becca to the soldiers ward, remove any all of their belongings that would expose them as such," I instructed.

"But what if they go down there and…." Rose pretested.

"We cannot worry about that we just need to do what we can, hurry up and go! Go! They will be here soon," I demanded.

They all took off running down the hallway removing all signs that could identify any soldiers in the hospital. Most had been stripped of their gear and clothing due to their injuries, but we still had a few who had who had arrived earlier in the day with parts of their uniforms remaining on their body. Another round of gunfire goes off, Marjorie returns to me, "okay all the children and babies are down in the basement with Tasha and Ethel," Marjorie said.

"Okay, I want you to go down there with them and help keep those kids quiet as possibly," I quickly told her, as she turned to head back, "oh and Marjorie, if you hear any gunfire take those kids down the tunnel and out the back through the hospital," I said to her.

Wide eyed without questioning, she agreed and sprinted back down the hallway. Becca, Abby, Rose and Martha stayed with me.

Suddenly the gunfire stopped, and we could hear German soldiers speaking outside. I grabbed the girls, "listen, they are going to come in here. You do what they say, you speak when you are spoken to. They are just here to look for any soldiers. When they find that none are here, they will move on, okay," I said to them all. Shaking their heads in agreeance, I turned to face the main doors, and 6 SS German soldiers walk through the hospital doors. Their SS Leader out in front followed by 5 more SS soldiers carrying Gewherb24 rifles in their hands. They Stop, just slightly behind their Leader.

We stood quietly and as still as possible.

"Controlled breathes," I thought to myself, don't let them see your fear.

Once the soldiers came to a halt, their leader walked forward towards us, smacking his tongue to his teeth as if he was using his tongue for a toothpick. He came closer to me, a little to close but I didn't react as it could cost me or my friends their lives.

"Wer hat das sagen?" He asked, "who is in charge?"

I spoke fluent German, "Ich Bin," "I am," I replied.

He smiled, showing his yellow crooked teeth, I could smell the alcohol on his breath, and he reeked of onions and cigarettes.

"Sie haben das sagen?" he replied, "You? You are in charge?" with an evil smirk. Then he moved in closing the gap between us even more.

"Ja," "Yes," I replied. Trying to hold my composure, calming my stomach trying not vomit all over him, from the stench that was coming off him.

"Wir Suchen einige soldaten," he said, he was looking for some soldiers, continuing "Wir erfuhren, dass sie heir behandelt wurden," he continued, and said that they were told those soldiers were brought here.

I shook my head..."Nien, Keine soldaten heir," I replied to him. "*No* there were no soldiers here. Sie konnen sich umsehen, wenn sie mochten?" I replied.

I told him he could look around if he would like. He gave me a side smile grabbed my face with his hand gripping it tightly.

"Niemand sagt mirwas ich tun kann." "No one tells me what I can do," he said, releasing his grip from my face. He ordered his soldiers to Spread out and look around: "Verteilen sies ich und schauen sies ich un ubersetzen!" He shouted.

They do so without hesitation, going into rooms, throwing things around emptying drawers, throwing papers on the floor.

I thought to myself, "Just stay calm and they will leave, please God keep us safe."

The soldiers ward wasn't marked, but if they had gone down the hallway just a little further, they would recognize who those men were and kill them, then kill us. Two of the soldiers were making their way towards the east wing. My heart started to race beating faster and faster as they moved farther down the hallway. They were about to hit the first turn, when sounds of gun fire rang out from outside.

One of the other soldiers standing by the door ran over to their leader and whispered in his ear, I couldn't quite make it out. Their leader keeping his fierce gaze on me, I held his gaze, making it clear I was not intimidated by him. He smiled, his ugly smile and said "okay, we are done here let's go." "Okay, wir sind heir fertig, los geht's." He turned to his men, they stepped aside as he walked out the door, then his men followed.

I let out a shaky breath trying to grasp my composer, tears filling my eyes, my hands were shaking. The girls and I all hugged one another, taking a few moments to get a hold of our emotions. Then we waited just a bit longer until we felt it was safe to go grab the others.

We put all the children back into their beds, by this time it was in the early morning hours. Shift changes were beginning to take place. We had briefed the staff from what had happened. I believed they wouldn't be back, but I still reminded them of the proper procedures in case they did.

Abby and I gathered our things and walked on home. The sky was gloomy, I did not snow last night, but as the faint light from the sun was trying to poke through the clouds, giant fluffy snowflakes were beginning to fall as we made our way home. We stepped into our house, set our things down on our small little dining table. Fished out some frozen soup from the freezer and began to heat it up on the stove top. Abby buttered some bread for us, then made us both a cup of tea. We ate our breakfast in silence. Our brains going over the trauma form the event that unfolded. Not quite ready to discuss what had taken place just hours before. After breakfast we both were in dire need of rest, we retreated to our bedrooms. I undressed from my nursing garments folded them up and stuck them in the laundry to wash later. I put on my nightgown, made my way over to my bed. I laid my head down, tears streamed down my face. Crying until my eyes felt heavy, and when there were no more tears left to cry, I drifted off to sleep.

# Part Two

# Chapter Sixteen
Aiden

*May 19<sup>th</sup>, 1944*

*My Darling love,*

*It's been nearly Five years since I have felt your touch and held you close. The days grow longer here, as spring comes to, and end and summer is approaching. We have moved from city to city pushing back the German regime. We have had much success, but that doesn't go without saying the countless lives that have been lost. I write from a muddy soaked field here in France. Spring rains will be ending soon, and summer will bring about warmer days. I don't mind the summers here. It's hot, but I prefer the heat over being brutally cold. The summers here, they remind me of home and all that keeps me moving forward.*

*I'm surrounded by constant death, the dead sleep silently in their slumber, something I have come to envy silence and sleep. God what I would give to have more than a couple of hours sleep without the loud sounds of bombs being dropped around us or bullets flying at our heads. Oh, what I would give to have a warm bed and you sleeping next to me.*

*I miss your smile; I push forward knowing I will be home soon. Don't tell Abby, but I'm worried about Jimmy; he seems to be incoherent these days. This war has had many effects on us all. I try and lift his spirits, keep him engaged and focus on our return home. We talk about old memories, but those thoughts only keep you sane for so long.*

*He stares off into the distance detached from his surroundings, disassociating from reality. I guess that might not be a bad thing considering the alternative. I hope all is well back home. I love you my darling.*

*Always yours,*
*Aiden*

I folded the letter up placing it in my coat pocket, ready to mail out when we arrive at base camp.

"Alright men, time to get up and move out. We got a lot of ground to cover and a few short days to do it in," I said to my men. I grabbed my pack and looked around for Jimmy, he was sitting on a log, lost in thought I presume. I gently tap his shoulder. "Hey there mate, we are starting to move out," I told him. He looked up at me blank stare on his face. Like no one was home. I grabbed his pack and helped get him up. "Come on mate, only a few more days and we will be at camp, hot food, some shite coffee and hell, maybe there will be showers, because you reek of fuckin shite," I jokingly said to Jimmy.

That seemed to bring him back, causing him to laugh a bit, "I don't reek as bad as your breathe stinks," he joked. There, a slight glimpse of the old Jimmy coming back to life. We gathered up more of the men, Nikola, and Harold 'Hunch' Burgees. I don't recall how he got his nickname Hunch, but he liked it better than being called Harry or Harold. So, Hunch, it was. We moved out, hours and hours go by, the road we took has been cleared of enemy troops allowing for a smooth ride into Carentan. The soldiers here have been anticipating our arrival. Once we had arrived, I ordered my men to get a change of clothes, something to eat and some very much needed shut eye.

We will be here waiting for our allied friends over the course of the next few weeks, this will be our home until we are told otherwise. I give my letter to the postmaster and then headed to an area where I can rest for a few hours before it's my groups turn to do their perimeter walk. I grab a change of clothes and some food as well, and some bath amenities, like a toothbrush and toothpaste.

I find a spot under cover on the pavement, I shave my facial hair, finish up my food and change my clothes, then brush my teeth. The sun was starting to come through the clouds, breaking away giving us a short break from the constant rain we have been enduring. The sun was warm, I turned my face towards the warmth and thought about what Saoirse had told me several letters ago, about us all being at her parents' house, and she could see me with our baby, laughing and playing. That thought fills me with warmth and puts a smile on my face. I grab my pack and fold it into place making it a pillow, then I lay my head down point my face to the sun thinking of you, Saoirse, my love.

# Chapter Seventeen
### Callaway

Captains Log
June 5<sup>TH</sup> 1944,

The Americans have joined the fight. The imperial Japanese navy air service had Surprised the Americans with a military strike. Bombing their naval base in Peral harbor, on December 7th, 1941. They destroyed 21 American ships many lives were lost. We got word within the few hours after it had happened. Since then, the Americans military has been pushing Japan's ships back, forcing them to retreat. Meanwhile we have been fighting alongside many American pilots here in Britain. Smart, determined blokes they are, they have as much hatred and pain to fuel their rage for war as much as we do. Our next mission, code name Neptune, is to go in and storm Omaha beach, in Normandy.

All hands-on deck! Ground, air and sea support. The Germans have occupied the beach making it difficult to push the line forward. We have been informed, the Germans have heavy artillery guns in place, overlooking the beaches. They lined the shores with wooden stakes, metal tripods and barbed wire. Which sounds like one hell of an on obstacle if you ask me. No doubt, we will be able to break through and have another victorious mission. Air support will be made up of American, Canadian and our own, British airborne soldiers. My crew, and several others, will be alongside the cargo planes dropping the soldiers in as air support. It will be one of our riskiest missions to date. I just hope me, and my men make it back to base safely.

The years of the war have taken their toll on me. I have Hardened myself to the new pilots coming in off of training. Greens is what we call them, those who have not seen combat yet. My crew, what was once made up of 15 pilots, 15 great pilots, have now been narrowed down to just us five original crew members. Still alive, Henry, Samuel, Jay, Tommy and me.

My crew had acquired 10 new men in the last week alone, or I should say boys, they were boys. Green as the fresh new grass that has grown from the warm summers sun. I walk out to assess my newest crew members.

"Attention officer on deck!" Lieutenant Jay Williams yells out.

"At ease, gentlemen" I said, "we have a briefing in the hanger tonight at 0600 hours to go over our next mission. I expect you all to be there promptly. My co-pilot Lieutenant Williams here will help you to your bunks and get you all squared away. Then I want you all to report to the hanger. Alright" I finished, saluting them as I made my way towards the tower. All my men standing at attention, "Sir, yes sir," they rang out in unison.

Henry was standing outside the towers deck. He handed me a cup of coffee.

"I thought you might have needed some for tonight," he said. I took a sip, choking a bit, burning my tongue, "oh shit that's hot," I winced. Henry laughing, well yeah you can see the steam off the top there. I smiled back acknowledging how unobservant I was being, my brain recovering at what I had just seen.

"Yeah, I don't see myself getting much sleep tonight," I continued "This is a big mission," I sigh stroking the back of my neck. "We are going to lose a lot of men tomorrow," I said to Henry.

The silence was an understanding between us both. This War has been polarizing with how many people have died. Both soldiers and civilians. The emotions alone, can get you killed if you allow them to get in your way, I told myself, so I have learned to turn them off and it's how I cope. Is it right, probably not but it is what has been needed of me to make I through this.

Henry and I walked over to the mess hall. We see Jay and Samuel sitting at one of the tables, grabbing our food and making our way over to them. Shortly after, Tommy walked in and sat down next to us.

"Fucking sevens hell, this is going to be one bloody shite of a mission, aren't it?" Jay said.

"Bloody hell, you wanker don't go jinxing it now, Shite, I got too much to live for after this bloody mess is over," Samuel laughed.

"It will all be just fine if you bloody blokes manage to do your job right," Henry joked.

"Well, I guess that leaves you out of this then doesn't it," Tommy chuckled.

"You shut your damn mouth their Tommy boy, at least I can hit my targets unlike you, you bloody cunt," Henry laughed,

"Oh, haha yeah right, keep laughing you meat cleaver. I have hit every single one of my targets," Tommy gloated, standing up grabbing his cock while laughing.

We all started to laugh, throwing our dinner rolls at him. I looked on admiring them all, they continuously made more jokes towards one another. My smile soon fades, excusing myself, leaving them to their bantering. Henry gets up to follow me, but I gesture him sit down and stay with our friends.

I walked back to my desk and finished up writing a few more letters. One to Saoirse and one to my parents. I make a few more logs in my captains book. A few months into the war, I had started keeping a journal of all the things I have seen Hoping it would help me navigate and learn to cope with my feelings. Help manage my pain of loss and keep memory of my friends both alive and dead. I finish up with my captains log and made my way to the postmaster.

The evening sun has begun to set, slight clouds in the sky indicating a storm is making its way on the horizon. Tomorrow this time, my crew and I will be taking off on one of the deadliest missions we will have ever endured.

# Chapter Eighteen
Henry

Operation Neptune has arrived. We fly out at 0600 hours. The weather finally clearing up. My nerves seem to be getting the best of me today, I don't know why, but today fells different. I try and focus on what I can going over my final checklist as I have done the countless missions before. We will be accompanying cargo planes dropping soldiers into Carentan, as they make their way towards Normandy. We will take out the bridges on the Orne River, North of Carentan on the western flank. That is our mission. I head to the hanger where my plane was undergoing some maintenance. I took some tough hits to my outer exterior on our last mission that messed up some of my wiring and caused technical difficulty.

"Alright mates, how's my girl doing here?" I asked Remy, the head of the maintenance crew.

"She's all in good shape. We rewired the hardwire and patched up the bullet holes none of which hit your main engines, so we are all in the clear there. I'd say she is more than ready for her next mission," Said Remy.

"That's what I like to hear. Thanks, mate, I appreciate it. Tell the others I appreciate all their help and go ahead and move her out. We will be taking off shortly," I told Remy. He nods and heads off to get her get her ready to be removed from the hanger; I head over to our flight crew and touch basis going over our flight path and target spots one more time. They seem to all be in good spirits nervous but excited and ready to prove themselves.

Calloway came up behind me just then, "You nervous for tonight?" he asked.

"I wouldn't say I'm nervous, but I feel something is off. I don't know Calloway... maybe it's just my bloody thoughts getting the best of my mind," I continued, "I just feel like this one is going to be different yeah know, not like the others before. Call it some weird fuckin sixth sense situation, but I get an unsettling feeling," I finished.

Exhaling Calloway said, "Yeah, I know what you mean. I have

had an uneasy feeling about today as well, but we can't let it rattle our brains. We both need to be levelheaded. For our sake and the crews. They look to the both of us to lead them into this battle." Calloway gently patted my back, "Come on let's get on out of here get us some grub and go hang out with the crew for a bit, try and relax our minds before they send us into a spiral we can't fucking get out of," Calloway said laughing.

"Yeah, you are right I just need to relax, just another day another mission that's all," I said. We both walked over to the mess hall and got ourselves a nice warm meal before we head back to our planes for take-off.

We break off and I step into the cockpit, securing myself, I go through my checklist. Once cleared, I give a hand signal indicating all is clear for take-off to my ground crew. I start up my plane. I look to my left and see Calloway doing the same. I put my hand to my head and salute him, he does the same. We take to the runway and lift off one at a time into the sky, I can't help but I have this heavy feeling of nervousness from what's to come. "Stop it! Henry," I said to myself, "You got this mate, it's like all the other countless missions you have done before. Breathe in, and breathe out." I put my thoughts in check and refocus my gaze on the runway ahead. Lined with our flight crew of 15, among several different squadrons, waiting for the tower to give the signal, "go for take-off." The engines roaring, plane after plane taking off in a singular line, scattering across the sky Moving into formation as they reach their cruising altitude. This, right here, is the part I love the most. Seeing the evening sky filled with various planes filling the sky, gliding in unison. Falling into formation, myself and Calloway out front then 4 pilots on each side of us and 5 others flanking the tail, watching for enemy fire. We will fly through the night hit Carentan come early dawn. I look out unto the horizon, this thought I have managed to keep buried until today, but I know for some of us, this will be the last sunset and sunrise we will ever see.

# Chapter Nineteen
Abby

*March 27<sup>th</sup>, 1945*

*Dear Abby,*

*T*ime *seems to have halted since I have been here. I can feel myself fading into darkness. A hole, I find myself burrowing in and sometimes unable to get out of. I'm surrounded by death, never able to escape, everywhere I look someone, or something is rotting into the blood-stained ground. I try and hold on to memories of us, and for when the day comes, I get to come home and marry you.*

*I should have asked you to marry me sooner, I'm so sorry my sweet Abby. I keep thinking about all the ways I have failed you and I hope you find forgiveness in your heart for me love. I promise I will make it back to you, making you my Mrs. 's.*

*The other night as I fell asleep, I dreamed of some sort of epiphany. I dreamt of leaving here, being back home with you darling. The dream felt so real. I could feel your touch, smell your amber shampoo, like you were lying next to me. You are all I think about and dream about. The bits of you in my mind keep me from going insane, keeps the darkness at bay from consuming my every thought. You are my home, my safe place, you always have been my darling love. Take care of yourself and I will be home soon enough.*

*Eternally yours,*
*Jimmy*

Tears fell from my face; I fear I am losing him. I tell Saoirse as she reads jimmy's letter. She took my hand, "No, No Abby you're not going to lose him," she said, "They are all coming back to us, okay?" Saoirse grabbed a hold of me, hugging me tightly. I hug her back choosing to believe in the comfort of her words, that's all we have after all. "They are coming home" I say to myself over and over again.

We pray constantly for their safety, but prayer only goes so far in war. Saoirse gets up and heads to the kitchen to fix us both something to eat. I read the letter one more time and when I am done, I hug it tight, over my heart. I lay down on my bed, I close my eyes, and I see Jimmy's face. His dappling smile and Bright green eyes, his fire red hair. We are dancing in circles, he is holding me close, humming a melodic tune as we danced in circles. Two people becoming one holding on to forever, never wanting to let one another go.

The world is a cruel and unforgivable place at times. Makes it hard for those with the faintest of hearts to move through this world with ease. The weight it can bear, can make such a deep hole in one's heart. Too deep of a hole to climb out of and repair. That's when the pain grabbed a hold of you, grasping it in its hands and sinking you down to the bottom. If you reach that bottom, there is no coming back. I heard Saoirse yell from the kitchen, "Supper is ready," She calls out to me. I fold the letter up, kiss it and place it on my nightstand. I head on down to the kitchen, chicken soup for dinner again tonight. They have rationed our food even more these days. It's been harder to get supplies dropped in for aide. The hospitals are running low on medicine and bandages among several other items. We finish up our meals and change into our nursing gowns and gather our things for another night shift at the hospital. My body is drained, I'm running on empty. I know Saoirse is too, but it's not in her nature to say so if she was. She is much stronger than I am. She always has been. She's my rock when things go wrong in my life. She has been a constant comfort with Jimmy being gone. She lets me speak my mind, getting all the awful thoughts out of my head, holding me while I cry in her arms when I feel overwhelmed. I know you probably think, "how selfish of me?" I promise I ask about Aiden always. I know it pains her, the not knowing if she will ever see Aiden again. She may not express it often, but I know what she is feeling, there are just some things that need no explanations, this is one of them

After dinner, we cleaned up and readied for work. I put on a sweater; the summer nights have just cooled enough for a light sweater on our early morning walks home after our night shifts. They say with the Americans joining in the fight, they will help strengthen our fronts and bring this war to an end. I fear though, that it won't come soon enough.

# Chapter Twenty
Saoirse

I sit at my desk in my office and ponder the thought of how do you begin to start a letter, informing someone you love immensely that their parents have passed all the while being at war? Quite the opposite of what I want to write him. I had just only received the letter yesterday. It was postdated from over a month ago. Mail, as you can imagine has been a much slower process since the war has begun. I think about all the ways I can tell him, going back and forth on should I, or shouldn't I? I know he would tell me without hesitation, and so I begin to write…

*April 25th, 1945*

*My Dearest Aiden,*

*I wish there was a better way of addressing this devastating news, but as for now, this is the only way I can tell you, I'm so sorry to say my love, that your parents have passed on. They were killed during the series of bombings from last month's air raids. I'm so sorry my darling love, my heart aches for you knowing I cannot be there to comfort you during this time of grieving.*

*The letter I have here, contains the contents and details of all that had happened. I wish I had better news for you my darling, just know this that their pain is no more, and it is my belief to choose that they had not suffered, but passed rather quickly and most importantly, together. This war has taken so much from so many others already and now it has taken your parents from you. I hope you know how much I love you my darling Aiden. Even though I am not physically there, just know I am holding onto you now, tighter than ever my love.*

*Your darling love,*
*Saoirse*

Tears filled my eyes; my heart has been heavy as of late. I fear for there is no telling how much longer I can keep a hold of my composer. Calloway and I had lost our parents last December. This war has left many open wounds on our souls. My parents, were on their way into the city, bringing Abby and I some food from their garden and some clothes my mother had knitted and a few letters they wanted me to mail out to Calloway. The roads were typically safe for their travels, but as of late they had increasingly become quite dangerous. Every now and then German soldiers would be seen passing through in small groups across the countryside. Spy's perhaps, but dangerous nonetheless and a risk I was not willing for my parents to take. I pleaded with them to stay home, that Abby and I would be just fine. But as stubborn as they could be at times, my pleas went unheard, and they decided on coming anyway. I was at work, just finishing up my day shift, unaware of the tragedy that was to unfold.

*Mr. and Mrs. Dunn's final moments*

*Was a crisp winters morning, the fog looked as if it was floating on top of the grass, it was quite beautiful I might say. The morning was remarkably cold, much colder than the winters we have had before it had seemed. The frost on our windows glistened as the morning sun broke through the clouds. Calvin and I are gathering a few final items such as eggs, potatoes, bread, butter and some cuts of chicken, along with several pieces of clothing I had knitted for the girls. We get it all loaded into our horse carriage and made our way towards the city.*

*We headed out around mid-morning, the birds were finally out chirping, the warming of sun coming through the clouds has started to awaken the wildlife. We had made a quick stop to see a few of our neighbors. Checking in on them dropping off a few essential items, like medicine, food and any other goods we had that we could share with our neighbors. Calvin and I may no longer be working in a hospital, but we are still doctors, and there are people here that still need help, and their medical needs attended to. We had spent a little longer at The Donnelly's than we had liked, and knew we needed to make haste heading to Saoirse to make it back home before dark. Saoirse has been worried, for the last few times we have ventured her way, there has been word spreading amongst the country folk that German soldiers have been making their way through the countryside from time to time. We have yet to encounter any of them whilst on the road, and Calvin, my dear husband chalked it up as mostly foley and was not worried in the least bit. Saoirse still asked us not to come, if only we had listened to her things would have ended differently.*

*After we left the Donnelly's, several miles down the road we had come across a fallen tree in the middle of the road. The tree must have fallen from the harshness of the winter bitter cold we had thought. We decided to go around it as it was normal for trees to fall this time of year. As we made our way around the end of the tree, taking us out off the road into the fields edge, as we were moving back onto the dirt road, 3 men came out of the tree line just off to the left side of the road. "Wohin gehst du?" "Where are you going?" The soldier asked.*

*"Mein Mann und ich sind Arzte und bringen unseren bedurftigen nachbarn medikamente und lebensmittel." "My husband and I are doctors, and we are bringing medicine and food to our neighbors in need," I replied to the soldier, hoping, praying they will let us pass unharmed. The soldier looked at us both for a minute, then signaled for us to pass on by. "Danke" "Thank you" I said, as we were making our way pass the soldiers, the words I had spoken, had barely left my mouth when they raised their guns, and opened fire on us. Killing our horses first and then my husband. I was severely wounded, as I laid hunched over in our horse carriage, bleeding out. They ransacked our goods, taking all that they wanted, leaving just moments later. When I knew we were in the clear I checked on my husband to see if by some miracle he was still alive. Cold to the touch, I knew he was gone.*

*He had several bullet wounds in his chest and face. I fell out of the carriage and crawled off into the grass. I had several stomach wounds, bleeding out all over. I rolled myself over, looking up at the sky, I could see the birds that were flying high above, the ground was wet and cold, the morning frost was beginning to melt under my body. I thought of Calvin, Saoirse and Calloway. They say in your final moments of life you replay all your favorite memories. While I laid on the ground, my mind was flooded with beautiful memories of my family. Tears quietly fell from my eyes down the sides of my cheek. "I'm so sorry my babies." With my eyes growing heavy, I sent out a prayer for Calvin's soul, for my soul and for Saoirse and*

*Calloway's souls, to keep them both safe. My breathing faint and labored, I whispered, "I will see you soon again my darlings," then I closed my eyes forever.*

A few days after they had been ruthlessly killed, a man, neighbor of theirs had come knocking on my door. Removing his cap, he stood in my doorway telling me all that had become of my parents untimely death. He handed me a few of the letters they had written to Calloway, the ones they had wanted me to mail out. I thanked him kindly as he turned to leave, I shut the door and fell to my knees. Letting out a blood curdling scream, Abby came running into the living room, she saw me leaning against the door, clenching the letters my parents had written to Calloway, cradling myself, repeatedly screaming this was all just a bad dream.

# Chapter Twenty-One
## Calloway

BAIL HENRY, BAIL! BAIL! BAIL! I yelled into my mask as his wing caught fire as his plane was spiraling out of control. I saw him eject from his plane, his shoot opening. As soon as he cleared the sky and landed safely on the ground, I could refocus my mind back on our mission. I drew my line of sight and fired my gun, diving down straight towards the battery gun, taking it out in one fluid motion. "That's two, three more to go" I say to myself.

I started to come back around to take out the third battery gun, when my plane had taken several hits to my left and right wing. My left engine caught on fire first. I tried to shut the valve off, suffocating the fire, preventing the engine from exploding and sending me into a swan dive towards the ground, but then the right engine gave way, combusting into flames, my plane was spiraling down towards the ground. I went to eject from the cockpit, pulling the lever, but not before taking a metal scrap to my leg. Punching out, I watched as I saw my plane explode hitting the earth below me. My shoot had only partially opened, causing me to spiral fast, down towards the grassy field below.

Landing hard on my feet as I hit the ground, my legs buckling beneath me. I started to untangle myself from my shoot trying to get up fast, but when I applied pressure to my right leg, I collapsed to the ground immediately wincing in pain. I sat up and grabbed my knife from my pack, I made a slit in my pants, ripping them apart. I tore off a piece of cloth from my shirt and tied it just above my wound, using it as a makeshift tourniquet to stop the bleeding. The metal rod went deep into my thigh, just missed the artery, thank God. The tourniquet was tied, I looked around, assessing my surroundings. I was feeling a little from all the blood loss. I laid on my belly and started to army crawl further into the grass to give myself some more cover in case I take on any enemy fire. I had no idea what side of the river I had landed on, and making myself known in my disabled state was not something I was willing to do.

I laid down in the grass, trying to control my pain. I could feel myself fading in and out of consciousness. I tried my best to stay awake, but with every passing second that was becoming harder to obtain. Then, I heard my name being called out, a familiar voice in the distance drawing closer. I couldn't quit make it out at first, "Calloway!" The man called.

"Calloway, can you hear me?" he called again. Then I realized, it was Henry calling for me.

"Calloway where are you?" Henry yelled again. I try to sit up, but I have no more energy within in me. I think to raise my hand, hoping he can see it above the tall grass, then I heard someone shout, "There!" an unfamiliar voice shouts out.

"Over there, I see a hand!" another solider shouted. My hand, unable to hold it up any longer falls to my side, my eyes feeling heavy, I fear that these are my final moments, my eyelids unable to hold them open anymore, in the slight slits just before they shut, I see a face, I see Henrys face, and I smile just faintly knowing he is safe as I lose consciousness.


I wake up in a hospital, my leg wrapped and in a sling. My eyes peering open, heavy from the morphine no doubt. I look around trying to familiarize myself with my surroundings.

"Well, it's about time you are awake, I was beginning to worry about you," The nurse said with a smile. I rub my eyes, and she hands me a cup of water with a straw in it.

"Here" she said, "you need to drink some water, your throat will be a little hoarse from being unconscious, so be careful when trying to speak," she said. I sip the water allowing it to coat my throat. She was right, my throat was dry, I went to speak but my words were raspy, quiet, like a soft whisper.

"Where am I? How long have I been out for?" I asked her.

"You sir are in a hospital just outside the city limits here. And you have been unconscious for 4 days. It's a miracle you are alive, with all the blood you lost. But lucky you, you had some angels on your side," she said.

Thinking about Henry, I asked, "Has anyone been here to see me?"

"Yes, as a matter of fact a very nice gentleman has been here to see you. He had been here every day, watching over as you slept," she said, with a smirk.

"He too was here in the hospital, only for a few days, never to leave your side. Until He got orders to return to his unit," she told me.

"He did give me this," She pulled a letter from her pocket and handed it to me.

"Thank you," I said to her as I took it from her hand.

"You are welcome, now I'm going to go check on some of my other patients, keep drinking your water there and I will be back with your medicine and a tray of food. I'm sure you will be hungry after all that sleeping you have been doing," she said, turning around, leaving me to myself.

I waited for her to be gone, then proceeded to open the letter. To my surprise the letter looked as if it had already been opened and it was indeed not from Henry, but from my sweet sister, Saoirse. She had written in her letter that our parents had been murdered several months ago. My heart ached for her, for us, and of course for my parents. I know this was not an easy feat for her to write.

Tears streamed down my face as I finished reading her letter, upon unfolding Saoirse letter to me, tucked inside was another letter, I had hers a letter addressed to me, from Henry. He had explained received the letter by mistake from the postmaster before our flight. Unbeknownst to him, he had thought it was from Abby, not paying attention to who it was addressed to. He had started to read it, quickly realizing it was indeed not from Abby, but from Saoirse, informing me about the tragedy that had unfolded bestowed on my parents. He had folded it back up and put it in his pocket. He had explained why he held on to the letter, wanting me to stay focus and my thoughts clear. He knew that if he had given me Saoirse's letter before we had left, it would have caused me to potentially make a mistake. He ended his letter with and apology and telling me how much he loved me. I couldn't fault him for the decision he made. He was right, I needed to be in the right mindset for my crew's safety and for my own safety. I read Saoirse's letter once more, wiping the tears from my face, having a hard time believing that our parents were truly gone. This feeling of grief was unlike anything I had ever experienced. A different type of grief than when you lose a close friend. I know had a hole in my heart, a hole that can never be replaced. I folded the letters back up, placing them both back in the envelope, hanging on to the wonderful memories of my parents. Wishing I could be with Saoirse now, comforting one another in our grief.

I spent the next several weeks in the hospital, I had little mobility in my leg and was told I would not be returning to active duty. I got word I was going to be medically discharged, the thought of me going home while so many others were still out there fighting made me angry. I pleaded with them to let me stay, but was told I was no longer needed, that I needed to focus on getting well. I was awarded with the Purple Heart for my brave actions in the sky that day. I still had not heard from Henry, but I believed him to be more than fine and would write him upon my return to London.

I decided I was going to surprise Saoirse, instead of writing her I was coming home. I had arrived off the boat near London's port, I was escorted by military personal who drove me to my home. Pulling up to the building, I had all sorts of mixed emotions. Guilt, sadness, excitement, but overall, I felt a sense of relief. When I arrived, the driver had grabbed my bag out of the back, "Will that be everything sir?" he asked me. "Should I help you with your belongings?" The driver said.

"No thank you, I've got it from here," I said with a smile.

We saluted each other; he then got in his vehicle and drove off. I grabbed my bag and made my way up the flight of stairs to our flat. Wobbling, I was nearly out of breath once I had reached the third floor. I took a deep breath in and turned the doorknob. The door slowly opened. I was hit with the delicious smell of homemade chicken soup and homemade bread wafting through the air. I scanned the living room, no sign of Saoirse or Abby, I stepped in through the front door, closing it behind me. When I looked back towards the livening room once more Saoirse was frozen, as she stood there in front of me. Standing in silence for a few seconds, she then let out an excited scream and came running over to me, wrapping her arms around me. "How…how are you….how is this possible?" She asked me.

"It's good to see you too my sweet sister," I said smiling back at her. We stood for a few moments longer embracing one another. I have missed my sister dearly, being back home here, with her in these first few moments has made all my thoughts and emotions settle a bit. I dropped my bag and removed my cap, we walked over to the table and sat down. "Can I get you some tea, or something to eat?" She asked me.

"No, I am okay for now, thank you," I said to her. She sat down at the table, sitting across from one another, "So tell me, what happened are you okay?" Saoirse asked me. Hesitant to respond to her question, I felt a surge of anxiety rush over me.

"Yes, yes I am okay thank you," I said. I took in a deep breathe she could tell I was uneasy.

"You don't have to tell me anything you don't want to Calloway, I'm just happy you are home!" She said to me, reaching out for my hand. I grabbed hers, "Thank you Saoirse, God, I have missed you and Abby both so much. Speaking of Abby, where is she?" I asked.

"Oh, she is down at the market. She should be back her in a few minutes or so," Saoirse replied.

"Is it okay if I go back in my room and unpack," I asked her.

"Yes, yes of course, go, take your time and get settled in. Supper will be ready in about 40 min," she said. I got up from the table grabbed my bag and I made my way to mine and Henry's bedroom, everything was left perfectly in its place. Dust covered some of our portraits, but other than that, it was as if we had never left home. I unpacked my bag and cleaned the dust around my nightstand and off our portraits and bookshelves. Abby had made her way back home, upon her return, I heard a loud scream in the kitchen and soon after Abby, came running in and jumped into my arms.

"Oh, Calloway I am so happy to see you," she said, squeezing me tightly. I chuckled, hugging her back, "It's good to see you to Abby," I said.  Letting go of her embrace, taking a small step back, "Let me get a good look at you, yup same ole handsome Calloway as before," She quipped. We walked back to the kitchen and Saoirse had finished setting the table. We sat around, the three of us, saying a quick prayer, then started to eat our supper. The night went on, they asked several questions, such as what happened to me?  why was I sent home? I had explained my injury and what had happened, I was starting to feel a little more at ease as I was settling in some more. Abby asked me a few more questions about Henry, and if either one of us had heard from Aiden or Jimmy. The answer of course was not what they were hoping to hear. Truth is, I haven't talked, nor seen Aiden or Jimmy since the day we all left to our perspective units. I told her Henry was doing well, which as far as I knew he still was. We talked long into the night about our parents, Saoirse and Abby's time at the hospital, all and everything they have been through since us boys left 5 years ago.

"Alright my sweet darlings, I'm going to go to bed and get some rest. It's been a long while since I have had a decent night's sleep," I said to them both.

"Yes, of course go and get some rest we will both see you in the morning," Saoirse said. We all got up, giving them both a hug, I then made my way to my bedroom. I took off my garments and my dog tags placing them just under a picture of Henry and me. I pulled the covers back, crawled into bed, and I rolled over to Henry's side, his pillow still had a very faint scent of his shampoo. It wasn't much, but it was enough for me to feel at peace as I drifted off to asleep.

82

⚜

# Chapter Twenty-Two
## Henry

"I'm hit! I'm Hit! I'm taking on heavy fire; my left-wing engine has exploded. I must bail can anyone read me?" I shouted over the comms, but I get nothing but static response over the radio. The smoke was billowing, I needed to make a decision and make it quick. I grabbed a hold of a lever just below my seat and pulled it. Ejecting myself from the cockpit. Flying up out of my plane. My parashoot opens with no problems as I fall to the ground. Landing on my feet, I quickly cut myself-loose of my shoot. I gather my surroundings and move to take cover behind a brick wall that's only half standing, but it's enough to get my bearings. I grab my knife out of my back holster strap. My gun had fallen out from my bag while I was in the air. I slowly peer around the wall and listen, gun fire was going off in all directions, the ground and in the sky. I was right in the center of it.

I heard rustling coming from the bushes behind me, fully prepared to defend myself or die trying, I stay quiet as three men come peering around the other brick wall. I hold my breath, my adrenaline racing through my veins, patiently waiting for them to make their move. "Oye, you are alright their bloke?" One soldier shouted out at me.

"We saw your plane go down and came to get you before you fell into the wrong hands their mate!" the other soldier exclaimed. I exhaled, relieved to find that they were friendlies and put my knife down, "Thanks mate, I about shit me self-thinking I was on the wrong side of the river," I quipped.

"No, you got lucky their mate, all's good here" The soldier said. They handed me a rifle, "The names Nikolai and this is Johnson and Stevens," Nikolai said, "We are part of the 21$^{st}$ battalion.

I shook Their hands introducing myself, "I'm Henry, nice to meet ya," I said to them.

Just then I heard a loud bang and look up to the sky, I see Calloway's Plane explode in the sky above. I watch, as it all falls in pieces from the sky, ablaze, spiraling down towards the ground and explodes upon crashing, burning any last of its remnants. My heart sinking into my stomach, "Did anyone see the pilot eject?" I yelled out.

No response, so again I yelled, "did anyone see the pilot eject?" I shouted once more.

"I did!" Stevens said.

"Where did you see him fall?" I asked Stevens.

"Over there, straight out, over into the field," Stevens said.

"Are you sure you saw him land there?" I asked Stevens, clarifying his remarks, all while trying to hold my composure.

"Yes, I saw him land just there, about 50 yards from us," Stevens said.

"Alright, you three come with me. We are going to make our way North and see if the pilot is still alive. Stay on me, keep sharp and move fast. We will be exposed and out in the open," I stated.

"On my mark three, two, one, let's move, move, move" I shouted. Moving out 50 yards, slow and steady as we scanned our surroundings for any Germans that may be lying, taking cover in the grass themselves. When we reached the fields border, I halted the group. "Okay, move swiftly, keep your eyes out, pilots name is Calloway, or Captain Dunn. He may or may not be injured so time is of the essence," I said to the men. We moved out in 2 groups, fanning out, looking for any signs of Calloway, or his shoot. The grass was tall, up to my hip. It was going to take a miracle to find him, I thought to myself. I began to call out Calloway's name. "Calloway!" I yelled out, waiting for a response, but got nothing in return. just silence. I yelled again "Calloway!" "Captain Dunn!" I called again, and once more. I move my eyes over the tall grass, trying to find any sign of life. Fearing the worst, I turn when I heard Nikolai call out, "over here, I see a hand, over here!" he yells. I set my eyes to where Nikolai was pointing, and catch a glimpse of Calloway's hand, just before it fell into the grass. I run over to him quickly, when I reached him, he was losing consciousness, and his leg was bleeding profusely.

I could see he tried to stop the bleeding with a makeshift tourniquet. I grabbed one of the soldiers' packs, shuffling things around until I found some thick cloth and his morphine kit. I injected the morphine in his leg, next to the wound and proceeded to wrap it tight, hoping to keep him from anymore blood lose.

"Come one Calloway, stay with me don't fall asleep," I said to him. I can see his eye lids flickering, fading, as he becomes pale, losing color in his face from the blood lose. I check Calloway's pulse, faint but steady.

"Come on mate stay with me," I said holding his head in my hands, trying to get him to keep his eyes open, but it was becoming to be difficult for him.

"Shit!" I yelled out.

"Alright, Johnson come and help me pick him up, Nikolai take point and Stevens watch our six. We need to move Calloway out of here before he bleeds out get him a medic fast," I said to them. Johnson and I secure Calloway's body weight in between our arms, and I give the signal to Nikolai to move on out. We make haste through the grass, holding Calloway's life in our hands.

Sprinting through the field, we were almost to the half walled up brick I was at before, when I feel a sharp pain hit my side.

"Aw Fuck!" I shouted. With a deep angry breath.

"What is it?" Johnson asked me.

"Nothing, keep going we are almost there!" I exclaimed. We made it out of the field and past the brick wall. Nikolai, Johnson and Stevens, continued taking us to their base camp. Right as we arrived, I yelled for a medic. We laid Calloway on the ground; the medic comes running over.

"What do we got?" he asked.

"He took a piece of shrapnel in his right upper thigh. We tied it off just above the wound, he has lost a lot of blood and was already administered a dose of morphine," I said to the medic, wincing in pain. "Alright, you two take him to the vehicle over there. What about you? Have you been injured?" The medic asked me. I lift my shirt where the pain was coming from, dark red blood soaked my shirt where the bullet had gone through. Missing my internal organs, the bullet had grazed the side of my stomach.

"Let me look at you," the medic said. Pressing his fingers on my abdomen, I wince in pain.

"Aw fuck, that hurts mate! Might as well dig your fingers in there why don't ya!" I exclaimed in agony.

"It's a bullet wound," Medic said.

Yeah, no shite!" I said sarcastically. He laughs, focusing on my wound.

"Looks like it has gone straight through, I will need to clean it up and give you a few stitches, but it's nothing to worry about. Might be uncomfortable moving around for a bit but will be a nice scar once it's all healed up. You got lucky," the medic said.

"Lucky" I thought, sure if you want to call it that. He cleaned me up, bandaged my wound. They will stitch me up at the hospital.

I load up in the vehicle and head to the hospital with Calloway. He looks to be in bad shape, I pray he makes it through this. We arrive at the hospital, and they immediately rush Calloway off to have his wounds attended to, and I go into a separate area to be looked over myself. They clean my wound and stitch up my bullet hole, putting a bandage over it.

"You will be in some pain for a bit, try and take it easy if you can!" The nurse said to me.

"Thank you" I say to her. "Take it easy," I chuckled to myself. "Only if it were that simple," I thought.

When they had finished up with Calloway, I was able to go see him. "He will be out of consciousness for a few days. He is going to live. As for his leg, there was severe muscle and nerve damage, while it missed his artery, it doesn't go without say, that he will never be able to return to active duty," The doctor continued. "He will most likely walk with a limp, and eventually a cane, for support," he finished. I was having a hard time rationalizing the gravity of his injury, there wasn't anything left to say other than, "Thank you doctor, thank you for all that you could do," I said. He nodded, smiled and walked away. I pulled a chair up to Calloway's bed and sat down next to him. Wishing I could hold his hand, letting him know I was here I whispered softly to him.

"Hey handsome it's me," I said quietly to him. My eyes filling tears trying hold back them back, but to no avail. They fell quietly down my face, looking at Calloway, looking at his injury and so grateful he was alive. I don't know what I would have done if I lost him. I sat there for the next couple of days, hoping he would wake before I had to go back to our unit, or at least try and find our unit.

I pulled the letter Saoirse wrote to Calloway out of my pocket having placed the one I wrote him within hers. I gave it to his nurse when she had returned to care for his bandages. She agreed to give it to him when he woke. After she had changed his dressings and left us alone. I bent down, kissing Calloway's forehead, "I love you Calloway. I will be seeing you soon," I whispered. Wiping my tears away I turned to head back to my duties. I had the medic vehicle take me back to camp, the one I had come across a few days prior. When I pulled up and got out of the vehicle, I saw Jimmy and Aiden standing by the tent.

"Well bloody hell, you two are still alive," I joked walking over to them bringing them both in for a hug.

"Awe, it's good to see ya' mates. Both alive and both looking like

Shite," I quipped.

"It's good to see you too, Henry," Aiden replied. We hugged once more before Jimmy asked, "Where's Calloway?"

I had informed them of on what had happened.

"Sevens hells," Jimmy said,

"I'm sorry, brother," Aiden said.

"Thanks Mates, he will be okay, I'm just glad he is alive, and you two idiots are alive as well," I laughed.

"Come on, we got a lot to catch you up on now that you've officially joined our unit," Aiden quipped.

Over the next several months, I would be left in Aiden's 21st battalion. Several units had been made up of men from all military branches. We would go on to push back the Germans further. Moving from town to town. Weeks had passed, with yet, no word from Calloway. When I had arrived in a small German, I had received, a letter from Abby and Calloway:


*Dearest Henry,*

*I'm sure by now you have heard of Calloway's return home, but just in case you haven't yet, I wanted to let you know dear brother, that he has made it here safely. His return has brought much joy in mine and Saoirse's lives. We have been over the moon with his arrival. He seems to be in good spirits, but his demons still linger over him. Not unscathed of the horrors, his wound a constant reminder of how he is here with us and not there with you, unable to watch over you and keep you safe. He misses you dearly, feelings of immense guilt fill his mind. In time, he will heal, learning to forgive himself of the things he is not in control of. Soon, relinquishing himself from his burdens as you all will. We all have scares, it's about learning how to manage them, to keep on living in this world, cruel at times. He wrote you a letter, to you which I have placed within the contents of my letter. I love you my dearest brother, stay safe and stay alive.*

*Love,*
*Abby*

I fold her letter up and open Calloway's.

*My darling Henry,*

*I'm sure Abby has informed you I am home now. I should feel a sense of relief, but I feel immense guilt, and anger. I can't help thinking about how I am here, safe, while you are still overseas fighting and risking your life every day. I miss seeing your face, I long for the day you return to me, in my arms again. I will not drag this out too long and fill your mind with my overbearing thoughts and feelings. I do promise, I am doing well; I just miss you immensely. I love you, Henry. Stay safe, I eagerly await your return to me.*

*Always and forever yours,*
*Calloway*

"I love you too Calloway," I said, folding the letters up within one another and placing them in my journal. While I have my journal out, I took a few more moments to write a new entry.

*Journal Entry 34*

*October 26$^{th}$, 1944*

*We are moving out at the end of October. We will be Heading to Ardennes, between Belgium and Luxemburg. To take on the Germans there, on their western front. Hoping to push them back, I have great faith that we will prevail. I am proud to be in the presence of the 21$^{st}$ battalion. I have no doubt in my mind, we will end this battle with another successful mission in the books. I hope, with little life lost as possible.*

*Henry*

I placed my journal in my pack, then proceeded to make my way out to the Humvees. When all the men were loaded, we fell into line and made our way towards Ardennes.

# Chapter Twenty-Three
Aiden

Operation Neptune was in full effect. My platoon had moved on from Carentan and now, we are moving further towards Cherbourg. We took the port there in Cherbourg, on June 26th and from there, moved on straight into the city of Caen, on July 21st. We forced the German brigade back, after their failed attempt to conquer the city. By August 30th, we had taken back several cities and launched a second invasion on the Mediterranean Sea, near southern France. The liberation of Paris followed on August 25th, which forced the Germans to move back, and retreat east across the Seine. On August 30th this date marked the closure of Operation Overload.

After Operation Overload, a much-needed rest was given. We made our way over to base camp, eating, resting and restocking our artillery. I had received mail at camp, A letter from Saoirse, I was eager to read it as I had not been able to write to her for several weeks. It's hard to get mail out or in, but these past few months, as we moved further into Germany, Mail was harder to come by. I found a nice quite spot in the shade a building missing half of its side, it had just enough of the corner roofing to offer some shaded cover from the heat.

I opened the Letter, as I continued to read on my heart grew heavy. Like someone was bearing all their weight on my chest. Tears filled my eyes, I tried wiping them away, but I couldn't make them disappear. I finished the letter, took a deep breath in, trying to hold on to my composure, but failing miserably. I put my hands to my face and began to sob. My mother and my father, both gone from this world in a matter of an instant. A newly formed hole filled my heart shattering it into pieces. oh, Saoirse I can't imagine how she felt reading the letter and then having to tell me.

My heart ached for her and the burdens she has had to carry all on her own. I folded the letters up one inside the other tucking them inside my jacket pocket. I collect myself and head back to my squad.

"Nikolai, Jimmy, Henry and Stevens I need the four of you to gather the rest of the men and do a perimeter walk. Be vigilant out their boys," I ordered.

"Yes, Sir," they said, as they broke off to grab the others.

I went to go speak with Major Wallace, about our next heading. In the briefing the Major Wallace, had informed us we would be moving out to Ardennes in between Luxemburg and Belgium to fight the Germans on the western front. After my talk with the Major, I waited for my men to get back brief them on our next mission ahead.

"Alright men, we will be leaving in a few days making our way to Ardennes. Upon our arrival, we will be joined by multiple units to move in on the Germans. We leave at dawn, 0400 hours. If none of you have any questions to ask, then I suggest you all get some good rest tonight, for it might be a while before that happens again," I said. After the briefing I was able to break off and write a letter to Saoirse before I laid down and got a few hours of rest myself.

*My Darling Saoirse,*

*I received your letters love. Thank you, for informing me of my parents deaths. I know that was not an easy decision for you to make, but I'm glad you told me. I can't imagine how heavy your burdens must be, but know you are not alone. I am there in spirit, wrapping my arms tightly around you. I can feel you in my dreams, calling out to me, watching over me as I sleep. Just know, you are the reason I am alive and still fighting. I'm fighting to get back to you as fast as I can. I wanted to let you know that we are heading to Ardennes here in a Few days. I don't know when the next time I will be able to write you a letter, but do not worry my love, I promise when I am able, I will write you.*

*It won't be long before I see you again, I love you my darling Saoirse.*

*Forever and always your darling love,*
*Aiden*

# Chapter Twenty-Four
Saoirse

December 16th,1944, It's been 1,826 days since the war has begun. They split London's hospitals into 10 different sectors from the city limits out to the countryside. The most critical of soldiers and civilians would be taken to the hospitals around central London and the rest would be recovering in the countryside.

After my parents had passed, I had joined what they called the 'Skeleton Staff' which allowed me to travel from the London hospital with a group of other nurses and doctors, to transport those from our hospital to the hospitals located throughout the countryside.

This also allowed me to check on the country folk for any medical needs they may have. Most of the trips, went without incident, as the Germans were being pushed further back into Germany. England had very little, to no incidents with Germans crossing the countryside in many months, heading back to Germany, but on this day our routine visit to sector six would change our lives forever. We were partaking in our normal routine checks around the hospital in sector Six. Was a cold winter day, the sky was grey, and we had received several inches of snow over the course of a few hours, and we were expected to receive several more inches within the next few hours. I was usually gone three days on these visits. Takes about half a day of traveling out to the countryside from the city limits. Upon arrival, we immediately got to work attending to wounds and other medical treatments amongst the patients. Then, we made our way to perform some house calls, before heading back on home.

Most times, I made it back home around lunch time, except for days like today, when the weathers aliments would cause for a much slower pace, putting me home closer to dinner time. Today would have been no different, if they had not showed up at the hospital. I heard gunshots ring out from the tent behind ours. Sounds of blood curdling screams cried out for help. Panic, and fear was beginning to take a hold of everyone inside our tent.

I quickly gathered the nurses telling them to grab as many people as they could and run out into the trees to take cover in the woods. I sprinted out of the tent, looking around for any German Soldiers. I couldn't see any, signaling them all to make haste towards the tree line. As soon as they made it to the woods, I quietly made my way to the other tent. Shots were still ringing out from the tent behind ours; Making my way towards the other tent, the ground outside was covered in blood. Children's bodies lye dead, riddled with bullets. Doctors and nurses lye dead amongst them.

I felt a wave of nausea come over me, my stomach turning at the horrific site. I gently step around their bodies, trying not to step in the blood-soaked grass that surrounded their dead bodies. I made my way to the front of the tent, the gun fire had stopped, but I could hear soldiers speaking. I quietly, and gently pulled back the hospital tents front flap. It was already slightly ajar, when I pulled it back, I looked around in the tent. I kneel to the ground, getting on my hands and knees to crawl inside the tent, hiding behind patients beds. Rose and Martha's Bodies were lying on the ground next to the first bed when I had entered the tent. I covered my mouth, holding back the scream I wanted to let out. 2 of my dearest friends, violently murdered. I grab a hold of my composure, carefully making my way around their bodies to move further on in the tent. The soldiers backs were turned towards me, I could see there were possibly four or five inside. I moved just a little further, stopping when one soldier briefly turned their head around. I stay still, watching him scan the tent before he turns around again. Before I move again, I heard the German Soldiers speaking to one another. They were planning on executing every British and French soldier here, and the nurses and doctors who have helped treat them. I moved forward just a little further stopping just before the middle of the tent.

They then grabbed all the British and French Soldiers, along with several doctors, making their way out of the tent. I watched as I see, my friends walking in a line, heading outside to their deaths. I wanted to help them, but if I gave away my position, I too would be killed. After they made their way out of the tent, I peered out to see if I can see anyone that may still be alive. To my left, in the far corner, I see Marjorie, Becca, Tasha and Ethel lined up against the wall huddled close together. I stood up, I could hear the Nazi Soldiers outside. Giving orders, lining them up for execution. I stand up and make my presence known to girls. I run over to them, their eyes wide, and in shock to see me alive.

"How did….what….how did you make it in here?" Becca asked me.

"I ran out from the other tent before they had entered. Waited until the gunfire had stopped, then slowly and quietly made my way back here," I said to Becca.

"You could have gotten yourself killed! You should have run when you had the chance," Ethel said. Looking at the four of my friends scared, face soaked sweat and tears, "I could never have left you. Any of you," I said somberly. Tears filling my eyes, a lump starting to form in my throat, "Rose and Martha are gone," I said. Giving them a minute to internalize what I had just said before continuing.

"We need to be quiet and make our way to the front of the tent. Once there, I will look and see if we are in the clear. When I give the signal, we hall our asses to the woods alright!" I said to them. Shaking their heads in agreement, we all stood up to make our way towards the front of the tent, when there stood two of Nazi Soldiers. They had entered the hospital tent quietly when I was grabbing the girls. Looking at us smiling with their guns pointed at us.

"Where do you think you are going?" "Wohin denkst du, dass du gehst?" one soldier asked. He moved closer to me, grabbing my arm and dragged me over to their Colonel. I was trying to break free from his grip, but with each movement I made he squeezed my arm tighter. The soldier then threw me down on the hard, onto the ground.

"Get up" "Steh Auf," he ordered me. I slowly got up wiping the dirt from my blooded knees, When I looked upon their colonels face, blood drained from my face, when I recognized who he was. My heart beating rapidly in my chest, I kept calm, trying not to give him any satisfaction in knowing the fear I was harboring deep inside. I knew too, he had recognized who I was, for he smiled his ugly crooked yellow tooth smile at me.

"No soldiers here huh?" "Keine Soldaten Heir, hm?" he said with his ugly smirk.  I stared fiercely into his eyes as he ordered his men to take us to their vehicles. They Load us up into their vehicles and tied our hands together. I could hear the screams as they lined up the rest of our colleagues and executed them. I prayed the others who had made it to the woods, would remain unharmed and unfound. They placed us in the two separate vehicles, our hands tied together and placed potatoes sacks over our heads. They started to drive away and hot tears, burning my eyes igniting a newfound hatred Ione I have buried since the war had begun. As we drove away, I vowed if I make it out alive, I will kill this man, even if it means killing myself in the process.

We were taken from a vehicle on to a boat, I had a feeling I was no longer in England anymore. After what felt like several hours on the boat, we finally made landfall, still having the sacks over our heads we had no idea where we were. I just knew, I was no longer near home. They drove us to a building, we were separated, to place us into different holding cells. Prisoners of war we are now, traders to the German Forces as they saw it.

 We made our way down some steps, into a dark basement with minimal light shining through the cracks of the small windows, The ground was wet and water dripping on the walls. The air was cold and filled with a mildew smell, when they threw me into my cell, I lost my footing landing hard on the concrete floor. Scraping my already blooded knees open again. I pick myself up and brushed the dirt off my clothes, then they shut the door behind me. Locking me in here for good knows how long.

I made my way and sit on the damp cot, that's just barely lifted off the wet floor. I know Abby and Calloway will be worrying about me soon, I should have returned home by now. Oh god, the horror they are going to stumble upon when they go looking for me. I hold back my tears as I rub the palms of my hands on my thighs back and forth, taking in deep breathes, allowing for my brain to calm down from the horrific trauma of today's tragedies. I lay my head down and turn to the side, curling up in a ball holding onto myself tightly. I close my eyes and softly hum a tune to myself, anything to keep me from losing my mind. Silent cries coming from my friends, faintly echoing off the cement walls. We were ordered not to communicate with one another or else the consequence would be death. While humming a silent tune, my body shivers from the cold air, I think of a memory in hopes it will help me to fall asleep here tonight.

⚜

# Chapter Twenty-Five
## Calloway

"It's getting late" I tell Abby, as I'm steadily becoming more anxious.

"Calm down Calloway, you worry too much. Saoirse sometimes is delayed due to the weather or taking care of her patients. She will be home soon enough," Abby said with a tone of, 'I'm not entertaining your delusions'.

"I don't know if it's twin telepathy or what but, I don't feel right about this at all. I know you said she has been late before, but this, this feels different," I said to Abby.

"I don't know, I think we should go down there and see if everything is alright!" I continued, "what if something happened and there is no way she can get a hold of us or anyone for that matter? It would be at least another day to two before the hospital staff here, would send someone out to go check on them," I nervously replied.

Abby sat in silence knowing my fears were more than valid. She should have returned by now and that fact that she hasn't had my stomach in knots.

"Maybe we should drive down there? We would be there by morning. Even if it ends up being nothing and she was just held up, then at least we would feel better about all of this, laugh about how silly we felt. But I just can't shake this feeling I have, and I need to go and make sure she is okay," I said.

"You are going to feel so silly when you realize I was right, and you were worried about her for nothing," Abby said with a smirk.

"Please Abby, I don't feel right about this we need to go," I said "Okay, Calloway if you really have this sense of uneasiness, then let's go. Besides the worst Saoirse would do is laugh at us both, with our silly antics of worriedness," Abby said. Abby goes to slip on her shoes and Jacket, I do as well. We get into our car and make our drive out towards the countryside.

We passed by a couple Military check points just outside the city limits, then off straight away to Saoirse's hospital sector, sector six. On the way, my mind drifts off thinking about Henry and how he's doing. Not long after, those wonderful thoughts leave my mind switching to thoughts of Saoirse as we made our way closer to the hospital tent. With no sign of people or any vehicle trouble on the roadside, my sense of un-easement grows rapidly. It was supposed to snow many more feet tonight, the muddy roads kept the snow from piling up and cause for any car troubles on the road.

"Gosh these December nights seem to get colder as the years have gone on" Abby said.

"Ah, this is nothing love, just imagine sleeping on the ground as the snow dumps buckets over you, no fires because it will give away your position and get ya killed, and wearing the same old wet clothes, day in and day out since the summer. At least here, we have some heat in the car to keep us warm," I said with a smile.

"I can't imagine what you all have gone through, Jimmy has mentioned very little, bits and pieces here and there in our letters, but I know he keeps a lot of that locked up inside, in fears of worrying me," Abby said. Her head was down looking at her hands, twiddling with her thumbs.

"I don't know how much longer he can handle suppressing that darkness inside him. I wish he would talk to me and get it all out. I can take it, all of it, on for him so he doesn't have to handle those burdens alone," Abby said softly.

"He's going to be okay Abby. Jimmy, well Jimmy is strong and thick skinned. He knows you could handle it if he told you, that's not the reason he chooses not to tell you. He keeps it to himself because, no man or women or child should have to bear witness or hear of the unspeakable acts of what has come of this war. He knows you have seen your fair share of tragedies unfold and he doesn't want to talk to you about it because, he needs you to be the one constant thing in his life that isn't a daily reminder of the tragedies enclosed all around him. You are the one thing in his life that brings him joy, and keeps his mind sharp, and if he starts to talk about all the horrible things he has witnessed every time he writes you, then he isn't escaping from it, he is bringing it into the one safe place the war hasn't consumed," I said to Abby. Abby looks down at her hands again and nods her head, "you are right Calloway, I know when he is ready, he will talk to me about all of it. Until then I will continue remain the constant source of happiness and escapism for him," she said.

Abby turned to look out the window, the snow was falling from the sky, melting as soon as it touched the muddy water on the ground below. I empathize with her fears, and truth be told how you could one not? War is brutal, Saoirse and Abby have had their fair share of bombs dropped on them, Guns pointed to their heads and looked death in the eye many of times. It is the one thing we have in common, the shared horrors of war.

Winters morning light starts to peak above the sky as we approach the hospital's tent. There is an unusual silence, a sense of eeriness that hangs over the atmosphere. Pulling up to the tent outside, bodies laid scattered, with bullet holes riddled through the front and sides of the tent. I tell Abby, once we get out of the car to stay behind me. I grab for my gun beside me. Immediately, my pulse begins to quicken, this feeling of dread and despair begins to fill me as we made our way out of the car.

We walk towards the first tent. Looks like two Hospital tents, one here and the other just behind it. I signal to Abby to stay quiet and keep behind me. The first Hospital tent, there was no sign of Saoirse. Dead bodies all over the ground, patients killed in their beds. Innocent people of all ages. Abby and I look around for any signs of life. So far, as we made our way further back into the tent there was just body after body on the ground. We got to the end of the hospital; I see a hole has been cut open in the back. Abby and I proceeded through it, making our way to the other hospital tent. The front drapes were drawn and as I moved one side open, Abby looks over my shoulder and sees two of her friends, both nurses. She gasps and puts her hands to her mouth; tears begin to fill her eyes.
"That's Rose and Martha," she exclaimed. She turns to me, I hug her tightly, "Listen, it might be safer for you to outside and wait, there may be more of your friends dead inside," I said to her. Or worse, I thought, Saoirse could be lying inside. Abby shakes her head aggressively, "I'm not leaving your side, if Saoirse and the others are here, I need to know and I'm not going to wait in the car until you return to tell me my best friends are dead. I can handle this," she said. "Okay," I say to her.
"Are you ready?" I asked.
"Yes," Abby said nodding her head. After she collects herself, wiping her tears away, "I'm ready" she said.

We made our way through the tent; there was an immense amount of blood, like the first tent. Children of all ages, mothers, fathers, the elderly, all dead. We continue towards the back of the hospital tent. our way through no sign of Saoirse and the others. Looking around, their lye several dead doctors, nurses and soldiers.

We walked back through the tent and walked around to the side, in a line, bodies laid, each one having been executed. I told Abby to wait here as I went and checked their faces. Scanning over them, there was still no signs of Saoirse or the other nurses.

We walked back to the car; this place has trees and woods in the surrounding area. I think to myself, "maybe some had escaped to the woods? Maybe Saoirse made it out and is hiding, waiting for help?" I call out facing towards the woods.

"Hello?" I yelled out, hoping to hear anyone respond.

"You think there are others out there? still alive?" Abby asked. "I'm hoping Saoirse, and maybe some of the others, ran off into the woods when they heard gun fire," I replied. We moved closer to the woods and called again, standing just at the tree lines edge.

"Hello, is anyone alive out there?" I yelled again.

"Becca! Saoirse! Ethel! Marjorie! Tasha! Anyone?" Abby called out. We stay quiet for a moment, listening for any calls back our sounds of movement. Before I go to call out again, we hear movement in the woods, the sounds moving closer towards us.

"Here we are here" a young woman yelled. She made her way closer to us, her silhouette becoming more visible, that of a young nurse. Quickly, we had noticed she was carrying a baby and had several other young and older children with her, along with another nurse.

"What is your name?" I ask one of the nurses. Nervous, she hesitates to reply. Abby steps towards her, "Her name is Elizabeth, and that is Evelyn," Abby said. When they had realized it was Abby, they gasped and made their way over to Abby, she embraces them both.

"What happened here?" I asked.

"We were doing our daily tasked, when suddenly we heard gun fire coming from just outside the tent behind us. Nurse Palo told me to take as many of the children as I could gather and head towards the woods I never…. She shutters trying to hold back her tears, "I never thought I wouldn't see them again," Elizabeth said.

Abby hugs her again, looking over at me tears filling her eyes, with the look of fear and panic setting on her face.

"Did any of you get a chance to see where they went? Or who all they took?" I asked.

"No, as soon as we were told to run, we took off and hid deep into the woods, waiting for anyone to return. Evelyn said.

"The gunfire went on for several minutes and then once it stopped, we braced ourselves for the possibility of them coming after us, but they never did," she continued, looking at Abby, "We stayed huddled together in the woods all night. We had decided to make our way back when we heard you calling out for any survivors. Did no one else make it out alive?" Evelyn asked, looking over at Abby, who then looked at me.

"No, I'm sorry everyone is dead. We found Rose and Martha in the back tent. Saoirse and the others, we still have not found them yet," Abby said choking back tears, Elizabeth and Evelyn started to sob as Abby continued to hug them both.

"Come on let's get you all out of here and go get you all checked out," Abby said.

We headed back to the car, "Alright then, let's move on out of here, shall we?" I said. Everyone here was dead. Doctors, nurses, most of the children, men, women, all have been slaughtered like cattle. Mothers laying on top of their babies trying to shield them from the gun fire. There was so much blood you could smell the iron in the air. I have never witnessed anything like this before, my fears of what I have seen had exemplified. I wanted to know what happened to Saoirse. She wasn't in either tent, neither were a few of her friends, 'They', whoever they are, must have been taken.

My stomach starts to turn, I stood bent over, just off to the side of the first hospital tent, bile spews from my mouth. Unable to control the nausea any longer. When I was finished puking, I slowly lift my head, and stand back to a full upright position, wiping my face from any leftover bile. I collect myself, and walk back to the car, grabbing my canteen and rinse my mouth out. The awful bile acidic taste sits heavy in my mouth. I rinse the water around and spit it out. Doing that a few more times, until I could barely taste the bile anymore. I helped load as many of the kids my car, then the rest in one of the other vehicles that Abby would drive. The drive back to London was long and silent. When we made it London, we drove over to the hospital there. Everyone was helped and placed into their perspective beds. Abby had informed the staff of what had happened to the others. Several gasps, then sounds of crying echoed down the hospital walls. After Abby has consoled the other nurses, Elizabeth and Evelyn and Abby hugged one last time, saying their goodbyes, then we both left the hospital and headed on home. Fear, raced through our minds as we drove back home without Saoirse.

When we got home, immediately we sat at the table, neither of us hungry, but still needing to eat, I warmed us up some soup and buttered some bread with a slice of cheese on it. Forcing ourselves to eat, afterwards, washing the dishes, then both headed to bed for the night. "Are you going to be okay Abby?" I asked. Knowing for well, neither one of us will be able to sleep soundly at all.
"Saoirse is gone Calloway; I don't know if she is dead or alive. My hopes are that she is alive, and we will bring her home soon, but my fear is she is dead, lying in a ditch somewhere. To answer your question, no, I won't be okay until Saoirse is safe and back home. I know you won't be okay either," Abby said, before turning to head to her bedroom. She was right, thoughts swarmed my mind, the fact we didn't find her was a good thing, but the fact that we didn't find her was also a bad thing. Not knowing what has come of her or what would come of her, was one of the scariest realms of possibilities to be in. Your mind wonders into the deepest and darkest of outcomes.
    I can feel she alive, is still here with me; I hold on to that feeling as a sign of hope. I laid my head on my pillow that night feeling a sense failure washing over me. "I wished Henry was here." I said to myself. I think of a fond memory, the two of us, Saoirse and I when we were kids. I close my eyes, and as the memory comes in, in full color of my mind, and smile at this wonderful thought.

# Chapter Twenty-six
Saoirse

By what little light that shines through the small window where the ceiling and the wall meet, I have gauged, I have been down here for at least 3 days. We have no bathrooms. I am forced to do my toiletry business in the corner of my cell. The Nazi Soldiers all have but given us a half cup of water and nothing to eat. I can feel my body begin to weaken. I try and stay positive, focus my energy on the fact that I am still alive. I have imagined Calloway and Abby have made their way out to our Hospital Tents upon by now. Gosh, I cannot even begin to fathom the horrific scene they would have stumbled upon. I just hope the few that made it out into the woods were able to stay alive. These winter nights grow colder, death will come if they are out there too long.

I sip on my water slowly, trying to savor what I can, water doesn't come often here. I place it down in the corner by my cot, the side I lay my head down on and leave it there until I feel the need to sip from it again. I heard the door open above, and footsteps recede down the stairway. I sit on my bed, hands on my lap and wait for whatever they have in store. Banging on the cell bars, trying to scare us, all the while laughing at us. They stop at my cell.

"You!" "Du!" one soldier said. Pointing his finger at me, while the other opens the cell door.

Two soldiers walk in, step to the side standing guard, pointing their guns at me. "Like I'm going to make a run for it," I thought to myself. Then other steps in, walks over to me, grabbing a hold of my arm and yanking me to my feet. His fingers, gripping tightly around my upper arm, squeezing it hard. I make a mental note, not to show any sign of discomfort, for he will squeeze it harder. They get off on hurting us. He pushes me forward and we walk out of my cell, down the corridor and up the stairs.

The light, blinding at first, causing me to squint and blink uncontrollably, adjusting to their surroundings. Once I was through the doors, the soldier standing there cuffs my hands together. We continue to walk down a massive hallway. Beautiful paintings placed on the walls, of several of them with different landscapes painted, I would assume of Germany, none of them look like any familiar places in England. The further we made our way down the hall, several more paintings of Hitler hung strategically down the hallway. Every 3 photos there was picture of Hitler. The last one at the end, had the Nazi Flag and Hitler's photo in one, gold framed, wrapping all around the painting. Gold chandeliers lined the ceilings. This, this was someone's home or, just a very overly arrogant, decorated Military Headquarters.

We got to the end of the hallway, I see these massive French doors in front of me, they open, there stood several SS Nazi Soldiers. One standing on either side of the entry way, then as you walked in 2 more placed on the inside of the doorway, one in the far corner to the left of the room, 2 others, standing next to what I would assume the man in charge of this place. We made our way into the room, two of the soldiers say something quietly to each other as we pass them by. I couldn't quite make out what they are saying, but one of them looks straight at me, and gives me an evil grin. My heart sinks into my stomach, afraid of what's to come, I hold my composure.

They stop talking when the man in charge excuses them from the room, leaving me cuffed and alone.

"Sit," he motions towards the couch. I do as he has ordered me to. Not wanting to upset the moral in fear of my life and the others.

"So" he begins in English, "I heard you were harboring enemy forces, treating them in your hospital? Hmmm?" He asked. I stay silent, until I am instructed to speak.

"Do you know what we do to traders? Those who go against the third Reich, our Beloved Fuhrer," he said, licking the salt off his lips as he eats crackers with caviar, and sips on wine poured from a gold colander, into a matching cup. I don't answer, I know it is a rhetorical question, he is trying to bait me, see what I know.

"We torture them, then eventually, we kill them, or they just die from their wounds," he said, letting out a grotesque laugh.

"Now I'm going to give you a chance to explain yourself, for why you had all those soldiers in your hospital. Hmm?" He said. I look up at him, making eye contact, there is no reason to lie, excuses won't work here, and he knows we have helped their enemy; I am a British nurse after all. My existence alone is enough cause to be killed. "Sir," I start off, "The reason for those soldiers being there is that we are a hospital, we treat anyone and everyone who needs medical help. It doesn't matter what side they fight for, my job, our job, is to help those in need. I am not in the habit of checking their uniforms and seeing who they fight for, when they are bleeding out on my table," I replied. He smacks his lips, cunningly smirks, "So you expect me to believe you had no idea of who these soldiers were or who they are fighting for? And that you just, cared for them out of the goodness of your heart?" he said.

"Yes, sir, I do," I said to him

"Hmmm, so are you calling my men liars then? He said condescendingly.

"If helping someone who is dying and brought in on our doorstep regardless, of who they fight for is a crime in your eyes? Then yes, I have committed treason, as you so eloquently put it. But, when severely wounded German soldiers in dire need for help, I set my own feelings aside and cared for them, because that is what we do. We don't question we just do," I said. I wait for his response hoping my bit about helping his men would be enough to spare my life, or whatever plans he has for me. After several moments have passed, he finishes his food, wipes his hand on a towel and sets it off to the side.

A maid then came in and took his empty plate and food remnants and walks out.

"Do you take me for some kind of fool?" He said, with a tone that of disdain. He stands up and moves towards me.

"No, No I don't sir," I replied. He sits down in the chair across from the couch I was sitting at. Stares at me right in my eyes. His eyes, cold, dark and empty.

"I should just kill you, you filthy whore," he said. I remained silent and I hold my gaze with his.

"You are a trader to the third Reich, our Fuhrer and to Germany. You are the scum of the earth, just like those filthy Jews we rounded up like cattle and burned alive," he said with a grin on his face.

"None the less I do believe you are being truthful to me about your help of some of my men. But..." he continued, my stomach turning into knots, "One of my fellow comrades said he had the pleasure meeting you a while back?" His grin grew wider, "He told me you spoke fluent German and that you were very...." he paused looking me up and down like I'm a piece of meat he wants. "Very beautiful," he finished. The bile in my stomach was starting to build, the palms of my hands were starting to sweat.

"Where is it that you said you are from?" He asked.

"Dublin, Ireland" I respond.

"Dublin, long ways from home, are we?" he smirked. He stood up, signaling for one of his men to open the door. The butler opens the door and in walked the same solider that had brought me here.

He gestures for the soldier, "Take her back to my cell." "Bring sie zuruck in ihre zelle," he ordered.

But not before grabbing my hair, pulling my neck back. He takes a big whiff of my hair, inhaling and exhaling, "Smells like peaches and vanilla, how sweet," he said, then let's go of me.

"Bring, her back to her cell, but first, take her to the courtyard. She must see how we deal with traders." "Bring sie zuruck in ihre zelle, aber zuerst bringt sie in den hof. Sie muss sehen, wie wir mit handlern umgehen," he ordered his men. We walked back down the hall, about halfway, then took a right, walked through the kitchen, which led through a door to the courtyard. Confused, I stood there, just outside the door it was pitch black out.

"Now, you will pick which one of your friends gets to live or die." "Jetzt wahlst du aus, welcher deiner Freunde leben oder Sterben darf." The soldier said laughing, flicking on the courtyard lights.

Just there, several feet before me, knelt Becca, Marjorie, Ethel, Tasha and two others I did not know. Dogs were barking on either side of them, several more soldiers had their guns drawn pointed at their heads.

"There are seven of them, and when I give the order, you will pick which one of them dies first." "Es gibt Sieben von ihnen und wenn ich den Befehl gebe, wahlst du aus, welcher von ihnen zuerst stirbt," he said, glaring at me, with an evil smirk on his face.

"No!" I yelled back. Fighting as hard as I could to get free from this soldiers grip, but with every move I made, he tightened his grip that much more around my arm. Fearing he would break it, I calmed myself back down.

A giant chain-link fence encased the surrounding yard 15 feet high, barbed wire, wrapping around the entire top of the brick wall. Soldiers, holding German shepherds trained to kill on command, stand there on either side of the fence yard. I felt a hard shove on my back and fell forward. Landing on my hands and knees, the soldier grabbed my hair, pulling it back hard. Forcing me to look at my friends, screaming at me to choose. "Choose!" "Wahlen!" He yelled.

My friends, hands tied behind their backs forced on their knees, had tears streaming down their faces. I made eye contact with Tasha, her smile was a comforting sight, she holds her gaze with mine and mouthed "it's okay," to me. I stood up, still unable to choose. I felt a hard painful smack on my back. One of the soldiers had hit me on my back with his rifle. The other continued to yell at me in German, "Choose," Wahlen" He yelled, again and again. I wouldn't choose! I couldn't choose! how could I choose?! I would rather die than choose the death of any one of my friends. I yelled back, "No I won't choose, you will have to kill me," I said, looking at the soldier dead in his eyes. Smirking, he let out a faint chuckle, then smacks my face, hard, with the back of his hand. I fall to the ground, the hit knocking me unsteady. I grabbed my face, tears filling my eyes, my face on fire and in pain. Another soldier grabbed me, lifting me to my feet.

"Alright you won't choose, then maybe this will help you make a decision." "In Ordnung, Sie warden sich nicht entscheiden, vielleicht hilft ihnen dies bei der entscheidungsfindung," he said, then gives an order to one of his men.

"Go get it," "Holen Sie es Sich," he demanded. The soldier nodded, went inside, in a few short moments he was back. At first, I couldn't quite make out what he was dangling, as I focused my gaze harder, I could now see he was dangling a baby, a screaming crying baby. He had it upside down, holding it by its one leg. The baby was naked, its cries echoing through the courtyard. He went over to one of their dogs and held the baby just high enough for it to be out of the dogs reach. The dogs were barking and snarling, foaming at the mouth, ready to kill this baby if given the chance. Inching closer to the dogs jaws, I screamed. "No! Please don't make me choose! Please, no I can't choose!" I shouted again at the soldier. The other soldier dangling the baby, moved closer to the dog "Wahlen!" "Choose" he said, calm and firm. I dropped to my knees, look up at the soldier, "okay, I will choose," I finally said. The baby still dangling, I look up and point my finger to Tasha and yell out her name. "Tasha" I sobbingly yelled out.

"Very good." "Sehr gut" The soldier said.

I look at Tasha, she was still smiling at me, she had tears streaming down my face.

"I'm so sorry Tasha, I'm so sorry," I repeatedly said. Tasha, looking at me with her kind eyes, "It's okay, be strong, don't let them break you! Do you hear me?" she yelled out to me.

"You are strong Saoirse; you all are, do not let them break you. I have faith you will make it out ali..." POP! The sound of the soldiers gun goes off, putting one bullet into her head, and another in her chest. I watch as her lifeless body falls onto the wet muddy ground. The soldier fired another five rounds into her body, as she lye there already dead.

Laughing the whole time, while we all sobbed. Shortly after, he ordered to have the others taken back to their cells. They grabbed the girls one by one, shoving them from behind, beating them if they didn't move fast enough. Screaming at the to stop crying. Before it was my turn to go back to my cell, he turned me towards the soldier who was still dangling this poor baby over their dogs. In all the chaos, I had drowned out the babies cries for help. The soldier looked at me,

"You should have chosen quicker." "Du hattest schneller wahlen sollen," he said, then gave the order to feed the baby to the dogs. The soldier threw the baby up in the air, its screams reverberating off the walls. Before it hit the ground, two of the dogs jump into the air one grabbing it by its stomach the other by its head, ripping the baby apart, all of them standing their laughing, as this baby was being eaten. Unable to control myself, I vomit onto the dirt, crying, while they laughed some more.

"Filthy Whore." "Dreckige Hure." One soldier said, kicking me hard in my stomach. I fell onto my side hard, hitting the ground grasping for air, wrapping my stomach with my arms. One of the other soldiers had lifted me up, walking me back to my prison cell.

One by one we were all led back to our cells, a single file line, no talking. I was the last one to be placed in my cell, the soldier, who had walked me back, was gentle when placing me on my cot. He removed the rope from my wrists. Looking away, I couldn't stand the sight of a German soldier, let alone an SS Nazi soldier. After he was finished with removing my rope, he tells me in a soft low voice "I can get you out of here." he said. Ignoring him, he repeated himself once more.

"I can get you out of here, you and your friends. But you are going to have to trust me," he said.

Feeling hesitant, I turn and look into his eyes.

"I will tell you more soon, But I can get you all out of here," he said, then stands up, his buddy soldier getting impatient.

"Let's go" "Auf geht es." The other soldier said. He gets up and leaves, closing my cell door. I heard their footsteps retreat up the stairs, when I heard the door close, I let out a blood curdling scream, I pull my legs to my chest and fall sideways on to my cot. I cry, and I cry until I have no tears left to cry. Beyond exhausted, thinking about what the soldier said, I couldn't help but feel a sense of hope. "What if he was being honest?" I thought. "He could be our only hope in getting out," I think to myself. I remained curled up on my cot. My head, pounding from all the crying and beatings from tonight. My eyes are growing heavy, I know I need rest, so I give in to the neurosis and finally fall asleep.

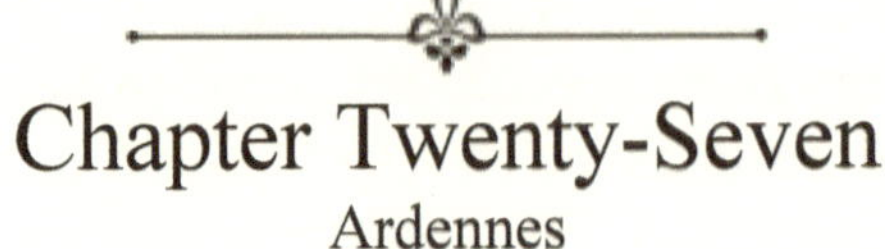

# Chapter Twenty-Seven
Ardennes


Aiden
December 16th, 1944,


Ardennes, is where the mouth of hell lies. Middle of December, it's so cold my hands, unable to thaw. I place them under my armpits for warmth. We lye in our foxholes, waiting, sitting, huddling together, trying to keep warm from the cold. There has been constant cloud cover over us for days now. This has not allowed aide to make landfall from our planes. The snow has begun to fall, once it starts it seems to never cease until springs first rain. The German Forces have separated our allied groups, scattering us all over these woods. This has allowed the Germans to encircle us. The eerie quietness the snow fall brings, makes me uncomfortable, putting me on edge, for nothing, not even a bird has made a sound.

We wait, there is lots of waiting to see who will fire first.

The foxholes we dug helps keep us safe from gunfire and artillery shelling's. I'm cold all the time. No fires allowed, we huddle close under what blankets we do have, trying to warm. The constant shivering makes it hard to fall asleep most nights. This morning, the Germans surprised us with a surprise attack. Artillery Shells rained down on us like hell fire. Startling us awake from our frozen slumber. Those out on patrol, were yelling at us to stay put, and don't move from our foxholes. The Artillery was dropping all over the place, left to right, in front of us and behind us. All we could do was cover our heads and pray our hole didn't get hit. I was in a hole with Jimmy and Nikola, when I was startled awake by the loud shelling's. Unable to move we braced ourselves for any impact or falling debris. Tress crashing down around us, one falling on top of our foxhole. Fearing we were unable to get out, we quickly looked around. We managed to find a gap, big enough for us to slide on out of our foxhole.

We started to run, I heard my name being called,

"Sergeant Palo, Sergeant Palo!" a solider is yelling out. I stop running and look around me, unable to make out who was calling me. It's loud, my ears are ringing from the bombs. Smoke fills the air, the once eerie silence I dreaded, was now filled with the loud sounds of Ambush fire falling from the sky above. I look around again, and I heard my name being called out once more.

"Aiden!" A familiar voice calls out. I finally see who is calling my name, it's Henry. I grab Jimmy, who then grabbed Nikola, and we run over to Henrys Foxhole. Barely making it, when suddenly an Artillery shell drops nearly 15 feet from us. The blast, forcefully throwing us into Henry's foxhole. He grabbed us by our collars pulling us into the hole. We assess each other, making sure nobody was hurt. This time, we are in the clear. We wait for what would be the longest 90 minutes of our lives. One shelling after another, you start to think to yourself, "will this ever end?" When suddenly, it stopped. Silence once again, calming the storm from before.

We wait for a few minutes, making sure it was safe to check on my squad. I signal for those around me to quietly get up out of their fox holes. Ordering all soldiers to check their surroundings and take a head count of who was still with us. I heard the calls out for the medics. Chaos, and screams, begin to fill the air. I lost 20 men, 20 good men. That's 20 more mothers that will be receiving letters, stating how valiantly their boy fought during the war, and what an honor it was to have him serve in the army. A letter, pre-typed and pre-signed by our Colonel. Yielding words of war, telling a mother her "valiant son" fought bravely and just how proud they should be of his sacrifices to our country. What a crock of shite that is. When in truth, the colonel, who sits in his safe space, eating and keeping warm, while these men fight on in hell. Every single one of my men deserves to have their stories told. On how bravely and valiantly they fought, but for now, I guess that letter will do.

It's a bloody miracle I have made it thus far. Sooner or later though death will come knockin, it always does.

*Jimmy*

*December 24<sup>th</sup>,1944*

*Christmas eve, what should be a wonderful, special time of year, is once again filled with death and suffering. A break in the shelling tonight, in honor of Christ and Christmas, there has been a call for a 24-hour cease fire. "In honor of Christ, and Christmas," as if they have some type of moral compass when it comes to the birth of Jesus Christ. How can you call for a cease fire on Christmas, but then continue killing all the other 364 days of the year? Bunch of shite is what it is.*

*Today the weather has decided to clear, allowing aide to be dropped in. Which I guess you can call that a Christmas miracle. I miss my home; I miss my darling Abby. The days never seem to end here, lack of sleep and the bitter cold has begun to fog my memory, a few men have been sent off the line and sent to a hospital. They are being examined for a term we call around here, "shell shocked." I don't know how much longer we can hold the line. My optimism has begun to fade and I'm slowly losing faith. But, if I can make it home, back to my Abby, then, that's the one wish I ask for, on this Christmas eve night. Every bit of fiber left in my bones, is barely holding on to the little pieces of joy and happiness, that once filled my everyday life.*

*I can't help that my mind, well it tends to go in and out of darkness. My thoughts, they are becoming unstable, drifting me further into madness, I fear, I don't recognize myself. I reckon, I don't see myself living much longer. I'm trying so hard to make it home to you, my sweet darling Abby, but my mind, God my mind, it's controlling the parts of me that I can't escape. The terror alone, I have never felt such an intense feeling of trepidation linger in me like this before. I'm so close to coming home, yet it still seems so far away. Your sense of being, it's what I long for, your reassurance that life, can go on and we will prosper, and I will be relinquished after this feat, but I'm having a hard time holding on to my sanity love, I promised I would fight for you, and that's what I will continue to do. Live to fight another day.*

*Henry*

*February 25th, 1944*

*A Lot of men lost their lives in this battle today, every day. Their sacrifice has led us to take back large amounts of the surrounding territories. Further, causing the German forces to reevaluate their positions and eventually, forcing their retreat. I sense, the war will be coming to an end here soon. After the "Bulge," we made our way on towards Rhine, taking on the Germans there, forcing them to continue retreating as we progress forward. There's Unwavering support amongst the men here, trying to keep each other alive, and our minds in the fight, so we can make it on home together. "No hero shit" Aiden repeats to us, with almost every other word that comes out of his mouth. Especially, before we head into battle. I don't know what the world will be like after the war ends. When we are back and thrown into our "normal" daily routines as before. The people who we once were, the young boys who were forced early on, to become men; we have all changed. Our minds, bodies and souls, the gravity of the horrors we have witnessed, the things we have been forced to do to other human beings, it's.... incomprehensible. No one, I mean no one, should be surrounded by this much death. We didn't start this war, but we will be finishing it, one way or another.*

*I miss Calloway, I miss my home and the life we had, until I see you again.*

# Chapter Twenty-Eight
### Aiden

*January 31<sup>st</sup>, 1944*

*My Dearest Saoirse,*

*I hope all has been well with you. I heard the Germans have been fully pushed back further into Berlin and that the Soviets, are that much closer to taking Berlin. I keep thinking about our life after the war, starting our family, and living at your parents farmhouse surrounded by cows, chickens, our massive garden, and our beautiful children in tow. I dream of that life with you, it is what keeps me going on the much harder days here.*

*Today, today was a hard day. We lost Nikolai. He was killed during our final days at the "Bulge." I sit here, writing you, trying to find the words to say to Nikolai's mother. A widow, she is and now a mother who has also lost her only child. There is no name to bear, for a mother who has lost her child. My guess is, the pain is too much for a name to be placed on a mother, or even a father grieving their child. Nikolai, he was her whole world, he was all that she had left and now she's alone. Jesus, I'm at lost for words Saoirse. I wish you were here to help guide me through this. You would know what to say to her.*

*I think about you daily, my love. My heart and my soul, I don't know how I would have survived this long without your comforting words. I will be forever enterally grateful for you. I love you my dearest Saoirse.*

*Love Eternally,*
*Aiden*

January brought more snow, more intense coldness and even more darkness than before. We had defeated the Germans at the "bulge," but not without the heavy loss of casualties. One of those being my good mate Nikolai. We took on heavy Artillery shelling's on one of the last few days before we had defeated the Germans on the western front. Nikolai's fox hole had been hit with one of those shelling's.

His body ripped apart, limbs removed, we wouldn't have been able to identify him, for his head was no longer attached to his body, just his torso was visible and his right leg. His dog tags had been tucked into his boot, the leg that was left lying next to him. I knelt next to the last remnants of him, reaching in his partially torn jacket to see if his letter he had written to his mother was still there, and to my surprise it was. I gently removed it from his breast pocket, placing it in my coat pocket along with his dog tags, dreading the fact I will be sending this back home to his mother.

Still kneeling I put my hand to my head pushing, my hair back taking a deep breath in and out trying to hold back my tears. Nikolai was one of my best mates. His mother was made a widow when Nikolai was a young child. His father was killed in an automobile accident when Nikolai was six years old. Changing a tire only a half mile from his home, his father was struck and killed by another motor vehicle passing by a mere freak accident.

His Mother, now widowed, was raising her son on her own, never to remarry. Nikolai was her world and the only child she ever had. Now he lies here, dead in pieces, spread about the blood-stained dirt and snow mixed. I stand up, and when I turned around Jimmy and Henry were standing just a few feet behind me. My face giving confirmation to what they already knew, both grabbing my shoulders, eyes glossy bringing me in for a hug. We stood hugging for a few moments, then wiped our tears away, we said a small pray for his soul and then got back to our duties. There is still a war to be fought after all.

This war has aged my mind my body and my soul. The boys we were, no longer exist. We became robots the day we started bootcamp, do as you are told, and ask no questions. Having turned into men over night, forced to shut off our emotions just so we can survive. You start to feel out here, that your odds of getting killed grow exponentially greater. Some days are much harder to cope, the humane part of you tends to break through those barriers that you have been holding back. The key to survival, don't give into your humanity.

The Russians have begun in talks of talking back more of Eastern

Europe pushing the Germans back once more. Italy has turned sides and joined forces with the Americans, forcing the Italians to surrender or retreat, that's the word traveling around here. We will be heading out continuing our move to the North, making our way towards Celle, Germany, a place I was fully not prepared for.

# Chapter Twenty-Nine
Abby

*February 26<sup>th</sup>, 1945*

*Abby's Journal*

Saoirse is still missing, I fear the worst for her, I can't help but think she is dead, lying in a ditch somewhere, and the animals scattering her bones across a grassy field unable to be found. The cold ground beneath her body, withered and torn. I pray for her soul if she should see death, I pray it came quickly without pain. But the truth is, that is unlikely. Those Nazi soldiers would have done horrible things to her body alive or dead no doubt.

I try and relinquish these awful thoughts from my head. How could I be thinking this way? I should be ashamed of myself for not believing she is alive. Tears stream down my face nightly. I'm trying to stay strong, stay positive for Calloway. He has so much more faith than I do. He keeps telling me he would know if she was dead. He would be able to feel it, somehow, I believe he is right. I feel, I would know if Henry had passed away. As twins, growing in the womb together, we form a bond that is unbreakable. We understand one another on a deeper level, Saoirse and Calloway would be no different.

But with every passing day she has not returned home, my thoughts grow darker. It has been well over a month since I have heard from Jimmy, no news is good news I tell myself. I fear I have begun to lose all faith in this world and in my own life. If I lose Jimmy too, then I won't be able to go on in this world alone without him. I'm not as strong as Saoirse was. I know it sounds silly, but Saoirse has always been the capable one in life, of the two of us. Jimmy, my soulmate in this life and the next, he has a way of making me feel seen. His presence has always brought me a sense of comfort in my life.

I pray nightly for their safe return home, Jimmy's, Aiden's,

Saoirse's and Henry's; I just hope my prayers will be enough to bring them safely back to us.

I'm weak with exhaustion, I have not been sleeping I'm up most of the night pacing in my room. Hoping Saoirse will walk through that door and tell me it was all a bad dream. When I finally do get some sleep, it's only for a few hours. My dreams are filled with nightmares most nights. Some nights though I get lucky, and dream of a memory that has come to past. Last night was a good night, I dreamt of Jimmy, Henry, Calloway, Saoirse and Aiden, the six of us together laughing, making dinner and telling jokes. It's a funny thing, how one day we are together in our living room laughing about our day, talking about our futures, just to have it ripped from your fingertips the next day.

"Abby?" Calloway calls out to me; I get up from my bed, putting my journal back in the drawer. Clearing my negative thoughts and head to the kitchen.

"How was the market?" I ask him.

"It was good, nothing new there of course, but I what we needed," Calloway said.

I nodded my head, forcing a smile.

"Can I get you something to eat or some tea?" I asked him.

"No thank you, I am okay for now thanks love. I have been meaning to ask you, how are you fairing? Have you heard from Jimmy yet?" he asked me.

"No," I replied somberly. "No letters today, I don't like that we have gone this long without hearing from any of them." I told Calloway.

"I don't know...I shudder a breathe trying not to cry, I swallow the knot in my throat, "I don't know how much longer I can keep staying positive as the days go on. These days are getting harder to focus and maintain an ounce of happiness or positivity. Calloway...I... I fear the worst. I try and stay mindful for you, for Saoirse, but I don't know how much longer I can do that for," I told him holding back my tears. He takes my hand in his and pulled me in for a hug. I sink into his arms a haven of familiarity, "I know love" he whispers, "I have a hard time staying positive myself" he continued, "But until I have proof of anything that states otherwise, then I will believe they will return home to us. I know it's hard at times, but don't think you have to hold it together all the time. I'm always here if you need to talk, or if you just need to sit and cry. Don't burden yourself with your feelings alone, you can always be honest with me. I'm here for you Abby, we are in this together," he said. He finishes, squeezing me one last time before kissing my forehead.

Calloway has always been a bonus brother to me. I know he is right, it's okay to be not okay all the time. That moment we had, breathed in a new sense of hope in me. That night, I prayed harder than I have ever prayed before, afterwards I laid my head on my pillow and began to dream of the family I have always wanted with Jimmy, that was the first night in a long while that I was able to sleep peacefully though the night.

# Chapter Thirty
## Calloway

Springs morning light appears through the see through shades that cover my window. I squint my eyes, opening them slightly. I'm just barely awake as the sunlight shines through the curtains. Yawning, I sit up in bed, rub my eyes and slowly get up to use the bathroom. I start the shower, it takes a few minutes to heat up, I step in letting the hot water pour over my entire body. Inch by inch my skin accepts the warm moisture so easily. I stand there for a few minutes before washing my hair then my body, faint sounds of laughter echoes down the hall. I can just barely hear it from the water rushing over my head. I lather up my body making sure every bit of me has been covered by the lavender honey scent the soap iridates.

Footsteps approach as I shut the water off and grab a towel. I step out of the shower drying my body off and when I turn around Henry is standing there just before me. Leaning against the door frame, his eyes gazing over every inch of my body taking it all in, he smiles and starts to walk toward me. He takes my body and pulled me in close foreheads touching, our eyes closed. I Take a deep breath inhaling his sweet almond, wood musk scent and when I open my eyes to look into his, but he is no longer standing there, and I'm reminded once again; that I'm back here, in our bed alone.

"It was only a dream," I say to myself, only a dream. I sit up in bed and get dressed. Abby is still sleeping, I quietly put my boots and coat on. I leave a note letting her know where I will be and how long I should be gone for, and I head out the door down to towards the market. Scanning the food items there, nothing new has come in. I grab what we are in need of, bread, milk, eggs and cheese. I put them into my bag after I have paid or them and made my way back to our flat.

My mind on the walk wonders from thought to thought eventually settling on Abby and how she might be fairing these days. Abby is a gentle soul, and I worry about her mental state as of late. With

Saoirse having been kidnapped and possibly dead, and no word from Aiden, Jimmy or Henry in months, I have this unsettling feeling, that something bad is going to happen and I can't shake it. I can handle any bad news that may come, but Abby, I am worried she could not.

Her fragileness, the despair and heartache this war has brought on could cripple her mental state. I can handle it for the both of us, taking on the burden, and carrying it for as long as I need to. I walk aimlessly thinking of every possibly scenario, other than the fact she may very well be dead. It's been 3 months since she has been gone and the very likely hood, she is still alive is nearly zero. I move on from Saoirse and Abby, focusing on something more positive. I think about the dream I had this morning of Henry and me.

I miss him lying next to me, waking up before him, Henry is not a morning person, his beautiful skin aglow in the morning light, His chest slowly rising and falling as he breathes in the gentle air. I slide in closer to him holding his body close to mine to remind myself this isn't a dream this is real life. He is mine and I am his. We hold each other for as long as we can before life's daily chores get in the way of our perfect moment.

I took a deep breath in savoring the memory, I am nearly home. I walk up the stairs in our building to our flat putting my key in the lock, I open the door to step inside, the room is eerily quiet. "Abby should be up by now," I think to myself, closing the door behind me.

# Chapter Thirty-One
## Jimmy

*My sweetest Abby,*

*We are nearly there, that much closer to me holding you in my arms. Gazing into those beautiful green eyes of yours and running my hands through your gorgeous, wild red curly hair. My mind has seemed to come back, and I feel like myself again. I am beginning to recognize who I am once more. All I do is think about you Abby, you've been what's keeping me alive, what's kept me moving and what has helped get me out of this dark, bottomless pit I was in.*

*I have this feeling our time is coming to an end soon. Call it whatever you want, but I don't think I will be making it home to you, my love. I know promised I would fight to make it back to you, but I may have to break that promise my love. I'm writing this letter to you as a reminder for how happy you've made me in my life, you have made me a better man, a better human being. Your endless, unconditional love I have received from you, has been more than what anyone has ever given me in my life.*

*Thank you for loving me, your warmth, that golden glow radiating from you the first time I saw you. That stunning smile, God it lite up the entire room. Gosh, just thinking about that very moment makes me smile. You were all I could see that night. My heart knew I would never ever be the same after having met you. I tried not to fall for you as silly as it may seem, I was scared as hell to screwing it all up and losing you forever. But you fought for me and for us. You taught me how to fight for love, what it means to be vulnerable, and understanding of each other's needs. You taught me love is worth fighting for, waking up every day choosing each other, no matter what may come at us. You changed my world, and I have never been the same, because of you my darling Abby. If I do not make it home to you just remember this, I won't feel any pain, anger or fear, I will only feel you, your presence over me. I had a dream last night, I was lying there on the ground taking my last breaths, I closed my eyes and when I opened them again, there you were laying on top of me inches from my face, those Firey red curls hiding us from the outside world. My hands on your face, your green eyes staring back into mine. I bring you in closer, getting a faint whiff of your perfume, sugar and vanilla scent from the light breeze blowing all around us. You whisper to me, "it's time to come home Jimmy." You start to float above me drifting further away from me. I lift my hand to reach for yours, but our fingertips are barely able to touch, you continue to drift further towards the sky above. I heard your voice again calling for me "Jimmy it's time to come home, my darling love." I stand to my feet, I see you in the glow of the setting sun, your hand reaching out for mine. I make way to you, running as fast as I can towards you, when our hands finally touch, I pull you in, holding your body against mine. I kiss you softly, whispering back to you. "I am Abby, I am finally coming home." Then I wake up. That dream makes me feel as if we will be together again real soon my darling love. I love you, Abby.*

*Forever yours,*
*Jimmy*

I fold the letter up placing it in a bag for safe keeping and place it inside my coat pocket. I wrote another letter and gave it to Aiden just in case my body gets blown to pieces, and my letter goes with it. We have continued on towards Landsberg, leaving this tiny Nazi town in its destructive path. We have captured several 100's of Nazi soldiers, killing those who have refused to surrender. Most of the Upper echelon has fled, but they soon will be caught and held accountable for their crimes or simply killed.

"Jimmy!" Aiden yells out, he was pointing at something just off into the distance. I look towards that direction, and we see several bodies hanging from a man-made lynching post. Men, women and children strung up from several different ropes and it tied around their necks hanging, them to death. For this is one of multiple lynchings we have seen, through these Nazi towns. They all had stars of David sewn on their clothing. I don't know what's that about, but sure seems to be used as an identifier for several of these poor people.

It's hard seeing humans hung and mindlessly beaten and tortured from the wounds and bruises. The children, my god the children having some of the worse markings on them than the others, tears fill my eyes as we gently cut them down, removing the ropes from their necks. We dig multiple graves and bury the bodies labeling them with makeshift unmarked crosses. After we are done, we continued to make our way to another town. Town after, town after, town it's the same old scene. Like living in a no man's land.

My stomach turns as this has been the worst one, we have seen. These poor people have been here for several days. The odor is strong, causing my stomach to squirm, I try not to retch up any bile. The crows have picked clean parts of their flesh. Their wounds, seem to have been more brutal than the others. We cut them down and carefully lay their bodies on the ground. Fly's and bugs alike buzzing around. I pull out a piece of cloth to help ease the smell and calm my stomach a bit. Other men around me can't help but vomit off to the side. Others, tears reeling down their faces, I know what they are thinking, how could someone or someone's, be so cruel, so evil, to do this? How could the towns people just watch it happen and not do anything about it?

Rage and anger fill my body, I feel the heat rising within me as I bury a small little girl, her hair still present, fiery red hair like Abby's and I can't help but think of the horrible things this poor child and many others have gone through. War is cruel, the ones who suffer the most are the poor, those unable to fight back. Taking the innocents and shredding it into a million pieces, then once it's over, it expects you to continue living on as if it never happened in the first place.

I dig the grave and set her tiny body in it, I place some flowers I had found in a field near by and say a small prayer for her soul. I fill the hole back up with dirt and place more flowers on top with a stone cross laying on her grave. I gather my pack, my gun, and we load up back in the Humvees. As we leave this town behind, I catch Aiden's gaze, he too has heavy feelings, but being our Sergeant, he needs to keep his mind clear.

After a few hours pass by, our truck suddenly comes to a halt. We are taking on immense heavy gun fire. A group of German soldiers coming up the over the hill just in front of us with a Panzer 2 tank. Small, but still big enough to do reprehensible damage. We spread out as the heavy artillery from the tanks gun takes out several of our Humvees. We take cover from the buildings just off to our right. We do an ammo and grenade count.

"Okay everyone takes a quick count of all your ammo and grenades," Aiden ordered out, above the thunderous sound.

"We have 200 rounds of ammo and 15 grenades," I replied, "Jimmy, Henry, you two flank right and get down into the trench there. Hold your position until you can run up and place the grenades on the tracks, enabling the tank on one side. When you are done, run as fast as you can taking cover behind the other Humvees. Don't be dragging your asses, get in and get out clean, you got?" Aiden said. "Yes, sir," Henry and I say together.

"Private Williams, Dickson, Johnson and Talarico, you four, flank left and take out the soldiers from the rear and eliminate those in the tank, the rest of us will lay down cover fire for you.

After you have successfully taken out the tanks, fall back take cover and begin to suppress a line of fire. We only have 200 rounds, so conserve your ammo and make your shots count.

Got it?" Aiden said.

"Sir, yes Sir," They said in unison.

"Alright men go on now, hey Remember, no hero shit, you hear me?" Aiden said firmly, Looking specifically at me.

"Yeah, I got it, No hero shit," I replied with a smirk. Henry and I leave, getting ourselves into position. Making our way down into the side trench, holding our position until we have the signal to make our move.

The others, getting into position, we wait, as the tank moves on down the road getting closer. We hold our positions, waiting patiently for the right time to strike. Not too early, not too late, we need to time it just right. "Just a little closer," I whisper, I give a hold position across the way to the other soldiers, "Steady, Steady……not yet, keep her coming...alright almost their sweetheart…alright okay…okay... now!" I yelled. Henry and I throw our Grenades, taking cover in the trench. A loud BOOM!!!! Goes off and disables the tracks from the tank. Henry and I both move on out of the trench, running towards the Humvees to take cover and lay down some heavy fire power.

Williams, Johnson and Dickson suppress heavy fire as Talarico climbs the top tank and drops a grenade in the hatch. "Grenade" Talarico yells out, jumping from the tank. Johnson and Dickson throw several more grenades behind the tank taking out the soldiers in the back and middle flanks. I see Talarico get up and run over to

Aiden, taking cover behind the building, falling in line and suppressing more heavy fire.

Henry and I have taken cover behind the Humvees that are still standing, just as I feel we are making headway, more soldiers are coming over the hill. "We don't have much ammo left; we need some more fire cover," I yelled to Henry.

"They just keep coming over that hill like Cockroaches!" Henry yells back laughing.

"I'm going to get up on the machine gun, we are taking on too much fire," I said to Henry. He looks at me, trepidation in his eyes.

"No hero shit! Get up there, fire out a few rounds and then get your ass back down here you got it," he firmly said to me.

"Yeah, of course mate." I smiled back. I climb up to the machine gun and start to suppress some firing.

I focus my firing mostly on the hill. Round after round, I stop and reload, and lay down more firing rounds, the gun jolts back with every round, POW, POW, POW as one after another is released leaving a deathly blow to those in its path. The sound around me goes quite as I draw out all the noise, focusing on the task in front of me. "One by one they all fall down," I say to myself, remembering the schools nursery rhyme. Suddenly, my gun jams bringing me back to the loud noises of gun fire all around me, I'm trying to fix the jam slamming the piston back and forth. Trying to wedge free whatever it is, stuck in there loose.

Finally, I get the bullet to lock in its chamber and I continue to fire some more. I see Henry to my right, firing from his position and for a moment I feel we might just make it out alive. I turn my head, focusing back on the hill when I feel as sharp pain lodge in my abdomen, then another one in my shoulder and another in my chest, I let go of the machine gun, putting my hand to my stomach. Blood covers my hand as I remove it.

I step back, my air becoming faint, making it hard for me to breathe as my lungs fill with liquid. I fall back off the Humvee straight down onto the hard ground. I see Henry, his eyes full of distress as he fixes his focus on me. He is shouting, but the noise around me has gone silent, unable to make out what he is saying. I lay my head back on the ground, I feel myself fading away, a cold feeling comes over me, covering my whole body. I see Abby's face come into sight, in the glowing sun. She's looking at me, smiling as she lays her body over mine. Her red, Firey hair, falls onto my face, our eyes meeting, just like my dream. I go to grab her face, her hair shielding us from the outside world. She said to me "it's time to come home, Jimmy." I smiled at her, Abby smiling back. I go to kiss her, but she starts to float above me furthering herself away from me. I reach for her, but I'm barely able to grasp her fingertips. "Come on Jimmy, get up my love, it's time to come home," she said to me. I stand up, and I see her in the suns warm glow. Her hand, it's reaching for mine, I hold it out in front of me, as I start to run towards her. When our hands finally touch, I pull her in close, our bodies touching. I put my hand to her face, Abby is smiling, looking into my eyes she said to me, "Don't be afraid my love." I go in for a kiss and for the first time, in a very long time, I feel free, a sense of peace washing over me.

"I'm not afraid my love, for I am finally home," I said to her, walking towards the sun together, finally going home.

# Chapter Thirty-Two
## Henry

"Jimmy!" I yelled out. I see him let go of the machine gun and grab a hold of his stomach. 3 more bullets fly through his body. "Jimmy!" I yelled again, he starts to stumble backwards falling off the back of the Humvee landing straight on his back. Blood spits from his mouth when he lands to the ground. I yelled for Dickson; he came sprinting over. He sees Jimmy lying on the ground, a pool of blood forming under and around him as he holds his stomach. "Dickson!" I yelled "Dickson!" I yelled again grabbing his shoulders snapping him out of his trance. "Dickson, I'm going to need you to take cover fire so I can help jimmy, alright?!" I tell him.

"Can you do that?" I ask firmly, he shakes his head and moves into my position, I bend down grab my med kit and administer a shot of morphine straight into Jimmy's leg. I took his coat off and pull up his shirt trying to find the bullet wounds.

As I lift his blood-soaked army shirt, I see 3 bullet wounds one to the upper chest cavity, 1 to the stomach and another in his left shoulder. He is bleeding from his mouth, his lungs are beginning to fill up with blood. He will bleed out to death if I can't get a handle on his wounds. "Come on jimmy," I said to him "Don't die on me mate. We need you buddy," I yelled at him, slapping his cheek trying to keep him awake as long as I can. I try to do what I can, but I can't get the bleeding under control. His wounds, especially the one in the chest, they are too severe, I can't stop the bleeding! "So much blood," I think to myself. The morphine has set in, his body is growing cold to the touch. Jimmy grabbed a hold of my hand. My tears hot, streaming down my face. I look down and Jimmy is pale white, shaking, he is whispering something, I can't quite make out. I lean in closer to his mouth, trying to make out the words he is speaking, but to no avail. I lift my head, focusing my attention back to his face. He is smiling at me, or maybe he is smiling at something else. He starts to raise his hand, "wait" he said in a faint whisper.

"Jimmy I'm here for ya mate," I said to him. He isn't looking at me but past me, he squeezes my hand, "Jimmy," I say softly, my face close to his. He turns his head slightly to me, "Don't worry Henry," he said, "I see her, I see Abby," he said with a faint smile, taking one last breath he said to me, "It's okay Henry, I'm finally going home."

His hand loosens its grip, his body stops shaking, and his breathing goes quiet. I sit back resting my bloodied hand on my knee, while still holding his hand with my other. I look out and see Aiden, unaware of what has just happened. Rage fills me, I hop on to the machine gun and start suppressing heavy fire on the hill ahead. I don't stop firing until I see no movement left on that hilltop, killing every last German soldier there. So many emotions coursing through my body. I step on down off the Humvee, Aiden makes his way over to me. He kneels by Jimmy's body, tears filling his eyes "I'm so sorry brother," he said softly, he looks up at me and with a gasping breath "I didn't keep my promise."

He takes Jimmy's letter out of his pocket and placed it in his. He grabbed his dog tags and his locket, inside it holds a picture of Abby. He grabbed his coat, shutting Jimmy's eyes, saying a silent pray before covering his body with his coat.

Standing up he orders the men to grab whatever ammo they can find and pile back up into the two remaining Humvees. We need to continue our course towards Landsberg. He looks at me, I already know what he doesn't have to say. We both turn to load into the Humvee, making our way towards Landsberg. We both stare out watching Jimmy's body fade into the distance, both of us filled with guilt, as we leave our friend, our brother behind.

The next several hours we all sit in silence, severely exhausted and hungry. "I can't believe I left him," Aiden said softly under his breathe. "Abby will never be able to forgive me for just leaving him there," he said. I listen, not knowing what exactly what to say back, "She won't blame you Aiden, you are being too hard on yourself mate," I said back to him. He nods his head in agreeance, knowing my words won't bring him comfort.

We drive on through the night and by sunrise we have made it into Landsberg, Aiden orders the men to get food, a shower, rest and a change of clothes. We are divided up and giving courters to stay in while we are here for what will seem to be a while. I too break off and head to my room. I took a nice hot shower; I haven't had one of these in months. I stand there and let the warm water rush over my body, tears falling from my eyes mixing with the water flowing down my face. My heart heavy from yesterday's loss. When I feel I have no more tears left to shed I shut the water off, I grab a towel and dry myself off. I had picked up a toothbrush and I vigorously began brushing my teeth for the first time in a several days, then I head downstairs to get some grub.

I finished up my meal and head outside to look for Aiden, he is nowhere to be found, I know he needs space, after losing Jimmy. I walk back to my room to write a letter to Calloway. I don't know how to start it or how to tell him Jimmy was gone. If I should even let him know. I don't want to burden him with possibly knowing before Abby does. Maybe I should write a letter to Abby, would be better hearing the words come from me her brother, or I should just let Aiden write her. If he chooses to do so. After all, Jimmy was Aiden's best mate and a brother to him.

The thoughts reel back and forth racking my brain. I decided I would just write, put the words to paper and if I send it home to Calloway then so be it or maybe I will wont, but at least they will be written down and out of my mind. Every loss, every new friendship that has been formed, all my fears, and worries, I just write them all down until my hand cramps up and I can't write anymore. So, I grabbed a pen and a few pieces of paper and did just that.

*April 4th, 1945*

*Jimmy is gone. Writing those words hurt more than I could bare. The realization that he will never be coming home, A promise we all made to keep one another safe has been broken. I have broken that promise. My soul once free spirited, full of light and hope, has been darkened with sadness, despair and guilt. Survivors remorse. What makes me so special, that I get to live on, and Jimmy had to die? A question I don't have the answer to and never will. I didn't know what I was going to say, or how I was going to explain my feelings to you Calloway, it pains me to know once you hear the news that I won't be there to hold you and comfort you, or Abby my dear sweet sister. I ask for her forgiveness, I tried everything I could to save Jimmy, but he his wounds were too great, and I was in the end, unable to stop the save him. He was incredibly calm under the circumstances; he found peace in death and that's more than what most men get when they die in war.  I don't know if I could ever look Abby in the eyes again, I have doubts that my apology will never be enough. If I make it home, how do we move on? How does our lives simply ever go back to normal? How do we simply forget? Memory is a funny thing, good or bad, imprinted on you like a tattoo, forever boding, once the ink has touched your skin, it becomes a part of you, you will carry it with you forever. Never to forget, but always be remined, our lives have forever changed, I just wish it was a more of a beautiful change.*

*~Henry*

# Chapter Thirty -Three
Saoirse

Ninety days have gone by, I make markings on the wall from a rock I found here in my prison cell. 90 days and 3 friends I have been forced to send to their graves. 3 souls that will forever live on, in my conscious. The tears stopped coming, before they would flow like a river streaming down my face out from my eyes, in a constant ever flowing state, but now nothing, just dry ducts and a depleting will to survive. The guards here beat us daily, getting off on our screams and the pain they cause us. The unnerving sense of dread that riddles our bodies, as they unlock the gate and enter our cells. Taking their turns one at a time. Clubbing us with their batons, fracturing our wrists, or breaking our fingers, one at a time. Kicking us in our stomachs, smacking us across our faces until our eyes are black and blue. Violently trying to break our souls with every kick, smack, and punch to our bodies.

At first, the pain would control my every thought. Unable to restrain my mind, I would wail and scream from the pain. Then that pain turned to anger, then to rage. Infuriated that I was here, that we were here. I felt as this was my fault, I should have done more, tried to bargain with them to leave us at the hospital or just to have killed us. Sending us to our death there would have been mercy. Every time I took longer to decide who would die next; the beatings would be far worse than before. Their minds are programmed to hate all and any who are against Hitler and his precious Third Reich. I loathed the Nazis more than I could have ever begun to imagine. This newfound repulsion I have, has kept me alive down here, some of the other girls haven't had such luck. Their pain and suffering, consuming their minds, has taken over their souls. Their will to live has left their bodies lifeless in their cells. Tasha, Ethel and Trisha, are all gone. Gone from this Earth, gone from this hell and free from this pain. Rest easy my darling sweet friends. I heard the door from the top of the stairs to open, loud heavy footsteps make their way down the steps. My heart begins to beat rapidly. I go and sit on my cot and wait for the soldiers to approach the cell door. His baton gliding over every cell bar as he makes his way down to the end. He stops just before my cell and turns to the one next to me. Orders one of his men to grab the girl. She starts to scream "don't touch me! Don't you fucking touch me ya filthy pigs!" She yells out at them.

I want to tell her to be calm and do as they, but she continued to fight, fight hard she does, until one of the soldiers cracks her over the head with the butt of his gun. I heard a loud thud as her body hits the floor. "Pick her up" "Heben Sie sie Auf" he yells at his men. I sit listening to the sounds all around me as they pick her up and take her upstairs. I don't know if she is alive or dead, but if she is alive, she is going to wish she was dead when she wakes up, if she wakes up. He then proceeds to come into my cell, and orders on of his men to grab me.

I stand up, and I go willing, as calm as possible, making their grip less tight on my arm. Out of the corner of my eyes I see the man who as claimed he was going to get us out of here. He falls behind the two men who are walking beside me and proceeds to follow me up the steps. His eyes, bright baby blue, his hair dark blonde almost brown which is odd for a SS Nazi Soldier, I thought, they usually have light blonde hair. When we reached the hallway, the soldier and his general are having a conversation. His general has gifted me to this man for his valiancy. Sick to my stomach from I had just heard, the soldier thanks his general and proceeds to takes me back to his room. I want to vomit at the thought of anyone touching me other than Aiden. I can feel my body heat rising and I start to mentally prepare myself for the worst possible scenario. He will rape me, repeatedly, until he is done with me then send me back down to my prison cell. That's worst-case scenario. Best case, once he is done raping me, he would then kill me putting an end to my suffering.

We get to his bedroom, he lets go of my arm, "I didn't hurt you, did I?" He asked me. Confused, I took a moment before I answered him, "No, no you didn't," I carefully replied. I don't know what game he is playing at, so I tread with caution. He locks the door and walks towards the windows, shutting all the curtains. He then turns to me and proceeds to tell me his name is Erik. I observe his demeanor, instantly, I get the sense he is not going to hurt me. He tells me he is a Russian spy, who has been working undercover as a Nazi SS solider.

I stood there in silence, taking in all he had informed me about him and what he was doing here. When he was finished, peering my eyes into his, "You could have helped my friends!" I said my voice low and filled with resentment and sadness.

"You watched for the past 3 months, while I have had to choose which one of my friends would die next? Taking the beatings, relishing in my pain, listening to their screams as they raped and brutalized the other women. And you, this entire time, you could have stopped them sooner?" My mind, seething.

"I needed time to figure everything out. You, and the others are not my mission. I am a spy; I relay any information I get and give it to my General. I'm sorry I have not acted sooner, but I couldn't have helped you then just yet. When I was able to formulate a safe plan to get you all out of here, then that's when I knew I needed to find a way to get you alone," he said calmly to me.

"You could have told your generals what was happening here! You could have helped us and saved them," I said, falling to my knees, putting my hands in my face, sobbing uncontrollably. All the pain, all the anger, all the suffering, it was now coming to the surface. I couldn't suppress it any longer. I felt weak, hopeless, crying in his presence. He stood there, not quite sure if he should say anything.

"I am truly sorry, miss. I have seen horrible things here; you are not the only ones who have suffered or in need of saving," he said to me. I know he was telling me the truth. I felt ashamed and selfish to think we were the only ones who have endured such brutality.

He walked slowly over to me, and crotched down next to me, "please miss," he said, sticking his hand out for me to take. He gently helps me up off the floor, "please understand, I wish I could have done more, but I would have risked my position, and I could not have done that. I know how you feel, the things......" he trailed off "the things I have seen and have not been unable to stop, all has been a test of my loyalty to the regime. I was not able to help you in those moments, but I am able to help you now, if you will allow me to?" He said. Of course, I was more than willing to do whatever he needed me to, to save the other women and myself.

I collected myself, wiping the tears from my face and walked over to the table in the middle of the room. Erik had pulled out a chair, motioning me to sit. I sat down, with Erik sitting across from me. Still unsure if I should put my full trust in him, but in my desperation, my willingness to live and make it back home to everyone especially Aiden, this man, Erik was my only hope at making that all come true. "Okay, so what do we need to do to pull this all off?" I asked him. He smiled at me, pulling out a map of the building, and from there we began to hatch out a plan to free us all from this hell hole.

# Chapter Thirty-Four
## Aiden

*April 5th, 1945*

*Dearest Abby,*

*I don't know where to start. The number of times I have begun to write out these words, are so many that I have lost count. I'll never truly believe them myself; the truth is there is no easy way to say this, and I hate I am having to write this to you. Abby, I'm so incredibly sorry that I must be the one to tell you, your wonderful, kind, funny, Jimmy, was killed in battle, on March 13th.*

*I still have a hard time wrapping my head around it all. He fought valiantly and with all his Irish gallantry, he braved his life for his fellow brothers in arms. I know nothing I can say will ease your pain. I do hope this finds you some comfort in knowing that in his final moments, Henry was with him. Henry had told me; Jimmy was at peace in his final moments. His last thoughts were of you, the words he had spoken before his passing, "I'm finally coming home Abby." I know I failed you Abby, and for that I am deeply ashamed.*

*I promised you I would bring Jimmy safely home, now I have broken that promise. I understand if you can never forgive me. I have placed Jimmy's locket you had given him, his dog tags and a letter he had written you, within this letter. Take care of yourself Abby.*

*Sincerely,*
*~Aiden*

I folded the letter up with Jimmy's letter tucked in between the folds, placing the locket and dog tags in the envelope. I Sealed it and sent it off. I was alone, sitting in silence in my quarters. I poured myself a drink and poured one for Jimmy, right as I was about to toast to him Henry walks in. Without saying a word, I pour him a drink and the two of us toast to our best mate. "Jimmy, for he is gone but will never be forgotten, you were an incredible friend, brother, fiancé and a remarkable solider. You fought bravely, as you always have. I wish I had half the courage as you ever did mate, you will be forever missed Jimmy, I love you," I said.

We tossed back our shots and poured another. Henry said a few words and after, we had a moment of silence, then tossed another one down the hatch. I sat down, my head started to spin a bit, with no food, the effects of alcohol have set in a bit faster than usual. "They have food being served downstairs" Henry said.

"Thanks mate, but I think I'm going to pass on dinner and drown my sorrows in this bottle, hopefully passing the fuck out," I said half sarcastically, back to him. He nods and sets his glass on the desk. "Alright mate, I'm going to grab myself some food, then get some rest. I advise you should do the same," Henry said to me before turning around and heading out the door.

I was alone, with tears filling my eyes, I pulled out a picture of Jimmy and I with Saoirse and Abby on either side of us, and Henry and Calloway at the end. Callaway had set up his camera to capture one last photo of us all together before we left. Even then, with all the worries and distresses we had before we left, there was still hope for our return. Upon arriving in this shit hole, we had naively thought wrong but continued to press on through it all. I watched so many of my men, friends of ours, die day in and day out, but I still felt we were untouchable. An ignorant thought, drastically proven wrong. No one is untouchable in war. We just had been lucky up until now. I recalled memories from our childhood, talking to myself as if Jimmy was in the room with me, laughing along at my stupid jokes. For a moment, I had felt he was here with me, and as momentarily that feeling came it was then gone in an instant, and I was here alone once again.

The best thing we ever did right in our lives was Saoirse and Abby. "Fuck!" I yelled loudly, pounding my fist on my desk. "Abby," I started to sob, "I'm so fucking sorry Abby, please! please! Forgive me!" I yelled out, begging for a forgiveness I would never receive. I broke my promise to her, and I will never be able to forgive myself for that. The next morning, I woke with a splitting headache. A knock was at my door, "Knock, knock," Henry said, as he opened the door with a tall glass of water, aspirin and a plate full of eggs, bread, bacon and fruit. I sat up slowly, my stomach turning at the acid that's left behind from the alcohol. "Thank you," I said taking the glass of water and aspirin first. He handed me my plate of food. "So did you drown yourself in sorrows and pledge you would seek revenge? Or did you curse yourself into oblivion and beg for forgiveness?" Henry said sarcastically.

"Yeah... something like that" I replied.

"Hmmm…... you can't go on forever blaming yourself Aiden. Jimmy was a grown man; he knew what he was doing. No one told him to get up in the Humvee and do what he did. That is not your fault, the sooner you come to terms with that, then you can begin to heal," Henry said.

"Henry…" sun was blasting in my face, causing my eyes to squint from the sensitivity my headache has caused. "I appreciate what you are saying Henry, but you didn't promise your sister you would bring her fiancé back home to her, alive," I said sternly to him. I found myself getting agitated with him.

"You are right, I didn't promise her that, I promised her more than that. I also made a promise to Calloway and Saoirse, I would bring you home to," Henry continued. "This is war Aiden, we made promises thinking we would be back in a couple of years, and we have been gone five years already. Those were promises made by boys who didn't know what we know now," he finished. "You cannot take on the burden of his death alone. I won't let you, and I know Abby, and if she was here now, she would hug you and forgive you before you even began to beg for it. My sister has no angry bone in her body, only love in her heart. I know she wouldn't hold us accountable for what we didn't, what we couldn't have known when we enlisted. You need to start to forgive yourself and let go of what we cannot control," he said patting my shoulder. "Now finish up eating and take a shower because you reek, we are meeting with the colonel in 20 minutes," Henry said.

"Okay," I said to him, as he walked out of my room.

I finished up my breakfast, took a shower and headed down to get myself a cup of coffee before I walked over for the Colonels briefing. "Good morning, Gentleman," the colonel said, as we all stood up upon his entrance. "Okay, you may all sit. Sergeant Palo, can you give us a quick debrief of your report. Colonel Marks said. clearing my throat, "We have pushed the Germans back into Berlin along with the Russians help and they are closer than ever to having access to Hitler and taking over Berlin," I continued, "We have had several reports come in that Hitler has retreated back within Berlins city limits," I finished.

"Are these credible sources Sergeant?" Colonel Marks asked.

"Yes sir, we have confirmed with several other reports that this is in fact factual information," I said.

"Great, thank you son," Colonel Marks continued. "Alright, your orders are to stay put here for a few more weeks then, you will move your men out towards Celle, Germany. When given the orders to do so," Colonel Marks finished. "You are all dismissed, except you Sergeant Palo," he said.

Everyone leaves the room including Henry, who is giving me a "what the fuck" look as he walks out and closes the doors behind him. "Son…". Colonel Marks begins, "Your last mission, I heard was a tough son of a bitch?" He chuckled

"Yes, sir it was," I said.

"I heard you handled yourself remarkably well under the circumstances," Colonel Marks stated.

"I would say I did the best I could under the circumstances that were given," I said

"Mmmm…They told me you lost one of your men as well," Colonel Marks clarified.

"Yes, Sergeant Owens was a remarkable soldier and fought bravely, he was……" I swallowed down the lump in my throat and continued, "he was my best mate, as well as my brother," I finished. Nodding his head, "I understand all too well of how you feel son. We have all had our fair share of loss, that goes without say," Colonel Marks continued, "I have a proposition for you, choose to take it, or stay where you are at, but I, and many others feel you are well passed do for a promotion. With your brave acts and leadership, I would like to promote you to Major Palo," Colonel Marks said, as he stands up and walks over to me. Stunned I didn't know what to say.

"Sir…I…," Stumbling to find the words, "Thank you sir it would be my honor," I finally said.

Colonel Marks then pinned my Insignia Patch on my Left Shoulder.

"Congratulations, Major Palo. It's my honor to give you this pin and well-deserved son," Colonel Marks said.

I saluted the Colonel and shook his hand, then he proceeded to walk out the door.

Henry came in after he left "So.... what did he say? Is everything alright mate?" Henry asked. With a puzzled look. I smiled and placed my cap on my head, pointing to the "Major" pin I was given. "Well fuckin bloody hell, you are a bloody Major now," Henry quipped "So does that mean you can stop moping around now?" He said jokingly. I punched his shoulder as he shook my hand, bringing me in for a hug. "Congrats mate, it's well overdue and very much deserved," he said. "Thanks mate," I said back, as we both walked out to go tell the boys and toast to my promotion.

The next morning, I had received intel that my men been informed of a possible secret base just outside the city limits here. They were told that SS Generals and Soldiers were seen leaving abruptly upon our arrival. I acquired a group of 15 men to do some reckon, see what they find and report back to me immediately if they stumble upon anything unusual. In the meantime, I had other things that were in need of attending to.

A few hours later I see Hicks, running up huffing and puffing, "Sir...." Breathing in and out fast "Sir, there's something...," he said again grasping for air.

"Alright settle down private, can we get him some water?" I yelled out." Another solider came running over with a canteen and handed it to Private Hicks. He drank the whole thing down in one sitting.

"You good now son?" I ask him. He nods his head "yes" then gives the canteen back to the other soldier and proceeds to start again.

"Sir, while we were out doing our perimeter walk, we came across something we think you need to see," he said calmly.

"Okay, private Hicks hop in the car and take me to this area you need me to see," I said. Private Hicks hops in and tells the driver where he needs to head. We proceed for about 10 miles outside the city, making a left turn into the heavy wooded area down a forest dirt road.

We followed the road for about ten minutes. Looking above the trees I could see they were starting to break and give way to the blue sky above. Getting a little closer, I refocus my sight back to the front of the vehicle, I see soldiers standing in front of what looks like a massive gate. It stood about 50 feet tall from what I could gather. Upon our approach, my stomach starts to form knots, and I get this unsettling feeling that this is not a base, but something much more sinister.

# Chapter Thirty-Five
Abby

April 10<sup>th</sup>,1945

My world is burning around me, my heart numb and frigid to the touch. I feel for nothing or for no one anymore. Everything around me in my life has shattered. My future turned into ashes in an instant.

I received Aiden's letter; one I have feared since this war had begun. My sweet, darling Jimmy has been taken from me. His words don't feel real. I clenched his letter as I fell to my knees screaming, crying, and praying this was all a cruel nightmare, but it wasn't. My body uncontrollably shaking, I am now alone in this world. Jimmy was my world. My soul mate. He was the part of me I had been missing, when our souls connected it was more than your average love. It was a deep, firey connection that went beyond just love. An eternal understanding of one another, the kind of love you would read about in fairy tales. But for me, it is here in the flesh, or at least it was.

Calloway has been by my side everyday doing his best to comfort me, but I am inconsolable. I love him for trying to help me. The truth is, that I don't want to move on or heal from this pain. The hole created in my heart is one I have never felt until now. I have survived my parents deaths; I have survived losing Saoirse, and not knowing what has happened to her was nearly unbearable. But I pushed through it and continued living the best way I knew how, But I can't survive this. My body may be here but my heart, my soul died the day I lost you Jimmy. I miss the way you would hold me when I was frightened. I miss the way you held my face in your hands before you would kiss me. Your sweet tender touches all over my body leaving everlasting imprints on my soul. You are the love of my life and the greatest loss of my life.

*Dear Calloway,*

*Thank you for all that you have done for me. please know that this is not your doing, do not carry this burden as this was my choice and there was nothing you could have done to change my mind. I love you immensely, my wish for you is that I hope you and Henry both live out your lives together, growing old with whatever happiness this world has left for you both. I know you and Henry will take care of each other. Remember, be patient with each other and give each other the grace that is needed for room to heal from the pains this world has brought on us all. This world may have taken the love of my life, but you two still have each other, and knowing that gives me peace.*

*Dearest Aiden,*

*Our dear sweet Aiden, I don't hate you. I could never hate you. I know you tried to keep your promise. But it was promise that was doomed impossible to keep from the start. A burden I never should have allowed you to carry. I know you did your best to keep him safe and alive. I know how much you loved him, and cared for him, cared for us. I hope you find peace and that you forgive yourself. I release you from your guilt, you don't have to carry it with you anymore. Just know we are both together now. This is not your fault either, this is my decision and one I would have made over again. You are a good man Aiden, the way you love so deeply for Saoirse, I know you understand just as much as anyone why I am doing this. My wish for you is that you find peace in your heart, happiness in your soul, and the find the will to heal yourself. Jimmy wouldn't want you to hold on to any anger or guilt, and neither do I. I hope you and Saoirse make it back to one another, never having to leave one another again.*

*My sweet Saoirse,*

*My best friend, the sister I never had but always needed. If you are alive just know how hard I tried to stay here in this life, waiting for you to come home. I, we never gave up hope on you. I know in my heart you will make it back home. You are much stronger than I could have ever imagined to be. I tried to make it in this world without you, but losing Jimmy pushed me into a depression I couldn't bring myself to get out of. My heart bleeding, with every beat, making a hole too deep for me to*

*bare. Your guidance has always kept me calm and has always helped
me take on this world, I am forever grateful for you. Thank you for
loving me and for bringing out in me, what I couldn't see in myself. I
love you my sweet sister, my best friend, my Saoirse.*

*Dearest Henry,*

*My beautiful, kind, sweet brother it has been an honor call you, my
brother. My twin. You knew me before anyone else did. A bond
unbreakable, created in the womb and forever entangled, your beauty
and strength radiated beyond anyone I have ever known, and I am
forever grateful for you. I hope you know I held on for as long as I
could. My heart already crippled from the death of our parents and with
Saoirse gone, Jimmy's death was the final blow. Please know Calloway
did what he could, but this was my decision, and I know all of you
would understand. My hope in life, is for you and Calloway to move out
to the countryside and live the life you two have always dreamed of. I
have faith that you will get your forever after and may you never have
to experience the unbearable pain of losing your soulmate. Just know,
that although I may not be here physically, I will always be watching
over you. I will be the wind blowing in your hair, the sunshine warming
your face, the voice in your head when you need guidance and in every
piece of earth you touch, I will be there. I was incredibly lucky to have a
brother like you to love and to be loved by. The best gift our parents
could have ever given me, was you. I love you, Henry. Be strong and be
brave.*

*I love you all and I am forever grateful for the friendships, memories
and love I was blessed with in this life. This is what I want so please
know it was never my intent to cause more pain and suffering. I just
wanted my pain and suffering to end. My final wishes are, that I would
like to be cremated and to have my ashes spread amongst the
wildflowers when you are all together again. Don't be sad for me, I
don't want any tears shed, for I am happier now and more at peace than
I have ever been. I am finally coming home to you my darling Jimmy,
and that for me is my serenity.*

*With all my love in the world,
Abby*

I laid the letters neatly down on my small desk. I placed the group photo on top of the letters, the one we had all taken before the boys had left. I went into my closet and pulled out one of Jimmy's favorite dresses of mine. Was satin blue, a pastel blue that had yellow, pink and green wildflowers spread out all over. Was fitted through the mid-section and was loose and flowing just below the waistline, cutting off just above the knees. Jimmy loved the way it looked on me.

I had decided on take a whole bottle of aspirin, for it was going to be shocking enough for Calloway finding me. There was no need to make it violent.

I waited for Calloway to leave for the market, that morning. I sat on my bed, and in front of me was a long dressing mirror. I admired my reflection, it being the last time I would be seeing myself alive. I knew if Jimmy could see me know he would think I was the most beautiful girl in the world. The thought of him brings tears to my eyes once again. I grab the aspirin bottle and proceed to take small handfuls at a time, on after the other, until the bottle was empty. I put the bottle on my nightstand and laid myself down on my bed, head on my pillow looking up at the ceiling, recalling all the fond memories of my life.

My salty tears falling down the side of my face, as my eyes start to feel heavy. Getting harder to hold them open, the pills are now beginning taking their affect, but I don't panic. My breathes, becoming quite faint. I can fill my time is coming to an end. I close my eyes for what will be the last time. I see a field of wildflowers, the sun is shining high in the sky, I can feel the warmth of the sun on my skin. Birds are chirping, I heard them in the distance, I scanned the field, looking for something, or for someone. I walk out towards the flowers, my hands gliding over the wildflowers as I walk on through the field. The sun was bright I had to out my hand to my face, help shield my eyes from the sun. My eyes catch something out in the distance. Focusing on a silhouette that is walking towards me. I think to myself I should be sacred, but I have this feeling of calmness and serenity about me. The silhouette becoming clearer as it moves closer. The shape begins to take form, a form I am familiar with, I squinted my eyes and when I readjust them, Jimmy's face appears. He stops just there before me. He holds out his hand, "Are you ready to come home My Sweet Abby?" he asked me. I took his hand, and he pulled me in close, I touched his face, running my hand over his body. I haven't been able to touch him in years. He grabbed my other hand, starts kissing my fingers gently, placing it on his chest and placed his hand on my face. I lean into him, my hands move, putting them around his waist, I whisper to him "I'm already home, my darling love." We kiss each other softly. My eyes having closed for the last time, I took my last breath and finally go on home to Jimmy.

# Chapter Thirty-Six
## Calloway

I woke up early and made myself some coffee. Abby was still asleep. The news of Jimmy's passing took a devastating blow to us both, but even more so to Abby understandably. As much as I tried to console her, I knew there was nothing I could do or say that would bring her any comfort. She lost her soul mate, and no words will ever be able to ease the pain, or fill the void left in her heart. I decided I was going to get up early and head down to the market and grab a few things for us. London was receiving more shipments of food and amenities. Still nowhere near what we have had in the past, but we were making progress.

Spring was in full bloom, the buds on the trees outside our house were beginning to sprout their flowers. Today was a mildly warm day slightly unusual for this time of year. I didn't want to be gone too long leaving Abby here alone by herself. I tossed back my coffee and headed out the door. Arriving at the market I had noticed a few new food items, Apples, bananas and oranges were stacked on the shelves. I grabbed a couple of each, then bread, milk and cheese. Small wrap of butter, a small block of Ham, some carrots, leaks, onions, and garlic. When I was in line to pay, I noticed they had received some chocolate bars. I grabbed two one for myself and the other for Abby.

I hope this would bring a slight bit of joy to her. She loves chocolate and has had a craving for it for months. The teller checked me out and I made my way back to the house, but not before stopping off at a local flower market, grabbing a beautiful bouquet of wildflowers. Abby loves wildflowers. I pay the man a few quid and start to head back to the house again. The sun was slightly poking through the clouds. I walk into the house, setting the groceries down on the table and begin putting it all away in their perspective places. The house seems awfully quiet, I thought. Either Abby is in the shower, or she is still asleep. I quietly finish unpacking the groceries, then I pull a vase from under the sink out and fill it with water. I cut the stems evenly of each wildflower. Arranging them in a beautiful bouquet inside the vase.  I place the vase in the center of the table then I go to grab the 2 chocolate bars and made my way to Abby's bedroom down the hall. I knock quietly on her door, waiting to hear any movement or calls back to enter, but i get no answer. I wait a few more seconds and then I knock again and still, no answer. I listen to see if I can hear the shower running, but no such sounds were coming from the bathroom.  I have an unsettling feeling in my stomach, she is awfully quiet and that is unusual of her. I knock one finale time, when I get no response back, I then go to open the door. Turning the knob, I carefully opened her door, my eyes fixating on a figure on her bed. My eyes registered faster than my brain, Abby was there, still as one can be lying in their bed. The dress she wore, the aspirin bottle on her nightstand, putting all of the puzzle pieces altogether, Abby was gone.

I ran over to her bed, grabbing her hand, it was cold to the touch, my heart shattering into pieces. I picked Abby up and shook her trying to wake her. "Abby! Abby! Wake up Abby!" I screamed, but I knew there was nothing I could do, Abby was gone, and her body was the only thing left of her. I sat in silence, as I held on to her, the tears poured from my eyes. I don't know how long I held her for, but it was a long while for, I wasn't ready to let her go. When my tears ran dry, I gently laid her back down on her bed, I kissed her hands then folded them together placing them on her stomach.

I get up from her bed and see the notes there on her desk. I grabbed the one with my name on it and walked out to the living room, sat down and began reading it. Every word I read broke my soul. Abby was in so much pain, more than I could have ever imagined. Could I have stopped all of this? The question I asked myself as I continued to read on, realizing no, I could not have stopped any of this. She lost the one person in this world that gave her life purpose for living. The moment she found out Jimmy was gone; her life would never be the same. Her soul unable to recover, she needed him and that's where she went. To be with him in the afterlife.

I folded the letter up and immediately thought of Henry. What was I going to say? How was I going to tell him? Should I tell him? The questions I asked myself as I sat at the dining room table lost in a daze. I heard a siren in the distance, snapping me back to reality, causing me to remember I needed to phone the hospital. I walked over to the phone and did just that. The ringing seemed like it was an eternity before someone answered the phone. A young women's voice finally answered the phone.

"Good afternoon this is Sara speaking how could I be of help?" Sara asked me.

"Hello Sara, is there a nurse Williams working at the hospital tonight?" I asked her.

"Hmm... let me just look at the chart and see if Elizabeth is on shift," she said. I waited a few moments while she checked the chart.

"It looks like she is working tonight, would you like me to put her on the line?" Sara asked.

"Yes, please that would be great. Thank you," I replied to her.

"Alright sir, just hold on moment and I will go and patch nurse Williams on through," Sara said. While I was waiting, listening to the hospital musical melody play on the line, I was trying to find the words to say, that Abby has passed away.

The a few minutes passed, felt like it lasted for a lifetime, then the music stopped, and Elizabeth picks up the phone.

"Nurse Williams speaking may I ask who is calling?" Elizabeth asked.

My throat felt dry, as I went to respond. My voice raspy, I clear my throat and speak again.

"Hello nurse Williams, it's me, Calloway Dunn, you may or may not remember me. It has been a while since we have last seen one another, and the last time we did see each other, it was not under the best of circumstances," I said to her.

"Yes, of course I remember you Mr. Dunn... how could I have forgotten?" She said, sounding so sweet and so happy. I hated that I was about to ruin her happiness.

Elizabeth and Abby had remained close friends after we had rescued both her and Evelyn that day.

"Miss Williams, there is no easy way to say this...." I began to choke back my tears as the lump in my throat seemed to be growing, I finally am able to get the words out.

"Miss Williams, Abby has passed away," I said to her, the phone, grew silent on the other end. I could hear her breathing heavily. "How..." she manages to stumble out a few words. "How did she pass?" she asked, sounding confused and upset.

"I had just spoken with her a couple of days ago!" She said. I explained to her what happened and how I had found her.

"I thought she… I thought she was going to be okay," Elizabeth whispered into the phone.

"I know, I did too," I whispered back to her.

"Miss Williams, I'm going to need someone to come by and take Abby's body back to the hospital and prepare it for burial service," I said to her, her sobs were heard through the phone as she responded, "yes of course, Mr. Dunn I will have someone sent over right away," she said.

"Yes, thank you Miss Williams." Before she hung up, "Oh and Miss Williams, you can call me Calloway, you don't have to address me as Mister Dunn. Makes me feel old," I said trying to comfort her a bit.

"Yes, of course Calloway. Thank you for letting me know about Abby. I can't imagine how you are feeling, if you need anything please don't hesitate to call," Elizabeth said.

I assured her I would be okay and thanked her for her kindness and condolences and hung up the phone. I waited in the kitchen for the coroner to arrive to take her body back to the morgue. My mind empty as I sat, staring off into oblivion. I jumped a bit when I heard the knock at the door. Three men entered. Two were hospital staff members Abby had worked with, and the other one was the coroner. They wheeled in a gurney. I had them follow me back to Abby's room. They picked her up off of her bed, placing her body gently on the gurney. "Do you know how she passed?" the coroner asked me.

"Ye…. Yes," I replied, "Ummm…. clearing my throat, "She took a full bottle of Aspirin," I finally said.

The coroner looks at me and then sees the bottle on her nightstand, confirming what I had told him. They took her down to the emergency vehicle, giving me their condolences upon their departure. Thanking them, I walked them out, would be several days before I would hear back from the corner. Shutting the door behind them, I walked over to the window and watched as they put Abby's body into the emergency vehicle, shutting the doors and leaving me here alone, with her beloved memory and the silence that would remain.

Once they were gone, I walked back to Abby's room and collapsed next to her bed. The tears streamed down my face once more. I was now alone and the one person I could lean on, she was gone. I lay curled up on the floor in the fetal position for hours. Processing today's tragedy, I knew I needed to get up, but I was finding it hard to get any motivation to leave her room. I know I need to write a letter to Henry, but my energy was low, I could feel my head throbbing from all the crying I had been doing. After another hour or so, I sat up and walked over to Abby's table, sat down, and there was a photo of the 6 of us amongst the other letters. Picking it up, I couldn't help but smile at the fond memory from this day. All of us were incredibly happy, untouchable, and naïve to the evil in the world. I placed the photo off to the side, grabbing a piece of paper and an ink pen. I took in a deep breath and let it out. Clearing my mind, I begin to write out the words I had never thought I would ever write.

*My Darling Henry,*

*It pains me to write these words down, but there is no easy way to tell you this. Our beautiful, sweet, kind Abby, had decided to take her life today. When Abby received Aiden's letter about Jimmy's death, it didn't just devastate her, it broke her soul entirely. No matter how many times I tried to pick up the pieces, there was nothing there to hold them into place. She tried her best to move through this world with a broken heart, her soul shattered, but in the end, she couldn't bear to be without him. She wrote out several letters, one to each of us, and then consumed an entire bottle of aspirin, placing her into and eternal sleep. She had waited until I left the house and went down to the market. She dressed herself in one of Jimmy's favorite dresses, laid her head on her pillow and passed peacefully. When I had come back from the market, I sensed in my soul something was not right and upon entering her bedroom, I found her in her in her bed. I knew right away before I checked for her pulse, she was gone.*
*I hope you know I had done everything I could have to make her feel loved and supported but some losses, make holes in our hearts too deep to repair. I love you, Henry. I'm deeply sorry.*

*All my love,*
*Calloway*

With my thoughts clear, I had decided to write out a letter to Aiden, he deserved to know what had happened to Saoirse. With Abby gone, I can no longer be the one holding onto these burdens by myself. They both deserve to know the truth. I'd never forgive myself if anything were to happen to either one of them, before I had the chance to be honest with them. I place both letters in the envelope, seal it and address it to where it needs to go. I will take down to the post office in the morning, and for right now I'm going to go back to my room and try to get some rest.

# Chapter Thirty-Seven
## The Camp

When we arrived, we were all unsure of what we were looking at. I get out of the humvee and walk past serval soldiers standing in front of the gate, blocking my view. Their silence unwavering as I made my way through the soldiers up to the gate. I Ordered one of my men to open the gate. They broke open the giant chain that looped around the gates lock. Many men, who surrounded the front of the gate were all dressed in the same type of clothing, that was tattered and heavily worn, you could tell that they had been wearing them for several months or much longer. When the gate was unlocked, we proceeded to walk in. So many of them standing before us, slowly moving backwards as we made our way on through the gate. One of prisoners, was asking us a question, I couldn't understand him, for I didn't speak any polish. But I knew one of my men did. I called out for Private Kowalski who spoke fluent polish and Hungarian.

"Private Kowalski!" I shouted over the other soldiers.

He came running up from the back, "Yes, sir?" he said.

"Private, I need you to help translate what this man is saying, if you would please do so," I said.

"Yes sir," he said again. Private Kowalski was to listen to the man's every word. The man was fragile, very gentle and soft with his words. There was a sense of fear in his eyes, maybe some confusion as well. I watched his facial expressions as Kowalski was speaking with him. "Jestes tutaj, aby nam pomoc?" the man asked Kowalski, if we are there to help them? I told Kowalski to tell him "Yes," and asked Kowalski to ask the gentleman, "what this is for and why they are here?" I said.

"Tak, co to za miejsce? Dlaczego tu wszyscy jestescie?" Kowalski passing on the questions to the man.

"To jest oboz I wszyscy tu jestesmy weizniami." "This is a camp, and we are all prisoners here," The man said to Kowalski.

Prisoners? I mumbled, ask him if they have committed any

crimes? "Czy wszyscy popelniliscie jakies przestepstwa?" Kowalski asked.

"Nie, nie popetnilismy zadnych przestepstw, jestesmy lekarzami, malarzami I prawnikami. Wszyscy zostalismy tu umieszczeni przez Niemcow." "No, we have not committed any crimes, we are doctors, painters, lawyers, we were all placed here by the Germans," the man said.

Kowalski, seeing the numbers tattooed on his arm and the star of David sewn on his shirt, Kowalski asked the man, "what were these numbers for on his arm?" "Po co byly te numery na jego ramieniu?" "Niemcy wytatuowali nam te numery na rekach, po tym jak sita usuneli nas z domow, dzielac nas- mezczyzn, kobiety I dzieci -do oddzielnych obozow." "The Germans tattooed these numbers on our arms after they had forcefully removed us all from our homes, dividing us, men, women, and children into separate camps," the man replied. Upon further questioning we had come to realize these poor people were brought here, starved, beaten, tortured and then left to die. Brutalized, they were left with very little water and no place to clean themselves or use the restroom. Kowalski and the other soldiers had started to hand out food and water to the men. All of them, you could see their skeletal outline underneath their clothes. They had deep sunken eyes, sores all over their bodies, wounds that were infected. When we walked further into the camp, we saw thousands of dead bodies lying all over the place. Flies buzzing around, I saw a man to the right of me holding what looked like a child in his arms, but it was no child, it was another young man whose body was so emaciated that he looked to be that of a child.

We called in several medics to our position, when they arrived, they had stopped the soldiers from giving these men any more food or water, forcing everyone to leave immediately, except for the prisoners. When they were examining some of the men, a rash was discovered on most of the prisoners. Further examination revealed typhus had spread throughout the encampment, these men needed to be quarantined immediately. Food and water would be slowly introduced into their diet. I had Kowalski tell the prisoners to move back and made all the soldiers leave. I sent Johnson and Hicks back to Celle to find a place we could place them all in for their care.

Not long after, we found a German Military school in town that was big enough to administer treatment for the remaining survivors.

There had been multiple diseases spread throughout the camp.

The poor conditions these people were forced to live in, was indescribable. We had never seen anything like it. We negotiated with the German soldiers we had apprehended when we arrived in Celle, to surrender. They did so without restraint. The camp was needed to be burned down, the bodies that were inside the camp were riddled with diseases and to prevent the spread of typhus everything must be destroyed. I then ordered my men to set the camp on fire, but before we did, my men had not only apprehended several German soldiers, but amongst them were several SS Nazi Soldiers. One, being of high rank. SS Haas First Commandant Heinrich Himmler, evil son of a bitch he was. He agreed to the surrender of him and his men, but before we were to burn down the camp, I ordered these Nazi Soldiers to bury all the dead bodies. At first, they hesitated. They knew they were sick and didn't want to touch any of the bodies. This was of their doing. Sick Basterds all of them. I lined them up and demanded they do as told.

"You are all going to go in to this camp, and dig as many graves needed, until every last body is buried. That's an order and nonnegotiable," I said.

SS Himmler started to laugh, "you expect us to take orders from a vile piece of shit like yourself? Hmm? You helped those disgusting rats when you should have left them to die, they are worthless, abominable, retched, filthy, disgusting creatures who have done nothing but cause problems from the moment they took their first breathes. Death is the only thing they are good for; A dead Jew is a good Jew," he said laughingly. I walked over to him, standing face to face, my eyes burning with fury.

"What's your name?" I asked him.

"SS Haas First Commandant Henrich Himmler," he said.

"You speak pretty good English for a German," I said.

"Yes, some of us do, me being one of them," Himmler said. "Hmmm, well how's this for some English." I cocked my pistol putting a bullet in the chamber and pointed it straight at Himmler's forehead right between his eyes. Very firmly, very calmly as clear one can be, "You will go in there and you will dig as many graves as it takes until every last body is buried. Or I will put a bullet in between your eyes," I said to him.

"You think I am scared of you?" Himmler said, smiling, showing his ugly yellowed teeth.

"No, No I do not. But I believe your ego won't allow for you to be killed by your enemy in front of your soldiers. So, I will tell you once more. You will go in there and bury those bodies or I will end you right here, right now. One last fucking Fritz on this earth, especially one as depraved, and diabolical as yourself. I wonder what your Fuhrer would think of you know?" I said, I could feel I was getting under his skin.

"I will give you to the count of three to decide." I pulled the trigger back ready to put a bullet in this guy's head. "ONE...TWO!" I let off a round firing it into the air, sweat peering down Himmler's face. I pulled back the trigger again, loading another bullet into the chamber once more and placing it back between his eyes. "THRE...." As I was about to say three, this fuckin cunt begged for his life.

"Okay, okay please, please don't shoot me! I will do what you have asked," Himmler begged. Smirking, I motioned for them to be placed inside the camp, locking them all in until every single body was buried. It took three days for them to dig all the graves and bury their bodies. When they were finished, we burned the entire camp down. Leaving no risk for the disease to spread we place the Nazi Soldiers in quarantine treating them for typhus, it was more than they deserved, but we aren't barbaric like them.

The Nazis had burned most of the prisoners' personal documents, burying any evidence of who they were, how many members they had in their family; nearly erasing their existence in entirety. We had come to learn there were four camps in total. One large men's camp and then a smaller one to the west of the one we had liberated. The women and children's camps were to the east and northeast of the town. They were liberated the day after we had liberated both men's camps. The women and children's camp were far worse than I had imagined. I knew it would be much like the men's camp. I was fully unprepared just how horrific their encampment would be. We brought back those who had survived, buried the dead and burned those camps down as well. We were able to reunite some family members back together, but many were not as fortunate.

I had designated soldiers who spoke fluent German, Dutch, Polish, Russian, and Austrian, to gather as much information as they could from the survivors. We were determined to reunite families and find out who these people were. The man I had met at the camp early in the week, I went back to check up on him and others. I brought Kowlaski with me to translate. Pulling up a chair next to his bed, Kowalski doing the same. The man was still very brittle and frail, but full of good spirits.

"I didn't get a chance to ask you your name," I said to him, Kowalski translating what I had said to him. He told me his name was Peter, Peter Nowak.

"Hello Peter, my name is Aiden, it's nice to formally meet you. How are you fairing?" "Witaj Peter, mam na imie Aiden, mito mi cie oficjanlnie poznac. Jak sie masz owieka?" Kowalski translated.

"Zyje ale tak wielu innych odeszlo z tego swiata. Wielu z nich bylo moimi przyjaciolmi," Peter said, "I'm, alive, but so many others are gone from this world. Many of whom were my friends," Kowalski translated to me. The guilt he has of living while many others had died around him was written on his face.

"We found the women and children's camp; we are bringing the survivors here now," I said to Peter, "There were several camps we had come across, many of those who had perished before we could get to them." I continued, "I tried to find your family based on the information you gave Private Kowalski before, and I have yet to locate them. Once we bring in all the other survivors, they will be medically treated, and their information will be gathered just like we did for all of you. My hope is to find them for you Peter," I said, Kowalski translating my every word to him. Peter gently grabbed a hold of my hand, looked me in the eyes, tears welling up in his eyes, "dziekuje za probe odnalezienia mojej rodziny, ae zostali zamordowani, zanim tu przyjechalismy." "Thank you, for trying to find my family, but they were murdered before we came here," Peter continued, "Zanim przeniesiono nas tutaj, bylismy w innym obozie. Moja zona Elena, moja corka Sasha, I moj Erik zostali wpuszczeni komor gazowej, a nastepnie ich ciala zabrano I spalono na popiol. Nigdy wiecej ich nie widziano I nie znaleziono zadnych dowodow na ich istnienie."

"We were at a different camp before we were moved here." Kowalski told me, "My wife Elena, my daughter Sasha and my son Erik were put into a gas chamber and then their bodies were taken to be burned into ashes, never to be seen again and no evidence of their existence," Peter continued, "Their memories will live on through me and will never die as long as I am living. Why I was left alive I may never know that answer, perhaps it's to live on and tell all those of the evil atrocities that had been committed here, I'm not quite sure, but I do know they have been spared anymore pain and suffering and are in heaven, and we will all be together again in time." "Ich wspomnienia beda zyc we mnie I nigdy nie umra dopoki ja zyje. dlaczego przezylem, nigdy nie znam odpowiedzi, moze chodzi o to, zeby zyc dalej I opowiadac wszystkim o zlych okrucienstwach, ktore tu, nie jestem calkiem pewien, ale wiem, ze zolstali oszczedzeni bolu I cierpienia I jestesmy w niebie, a za jakis czas znow bedziemy razem," Peter said to Kowalski and me.

Tears in his eyes Kowalski finishes translating for Peter. Peter pauses and takes in a deep breath, he thanked me, thanked us all for saving his life and everyone else that we had saved from these camps. I wished him well, getting up from my chair, Kowalski following, we walked out the doors, stopping just before the steps, I asked Kowalski if he was, "okay?" He turned to me pausing for several seconds, finding the right words to say.

"How can people be so cruel? So evil to another human being? How can they treat others as if they are nothing but animals they despise of? Where did we go wrong in this world?" Kowalski asked. I took my cap off and rubbed the back of my neck with my hand before placing it back on my head, looking straight into Kowalski's eyes, "I don't have the answer to that Kowalski, everything I have seen in this war since it has begun, up until this very moment, I thought I had all the answers for why some people do evil things. Most of it is easy to explain, when I saw those people, and the conditions they were in, I realized I knew nothing of the evils that live in this world. I have no answer as to why some humans can be so malignant. Just know that after we leave here, we will tell everyone what we saw in those camps. Details no matter how gruesome, the world deserves to know what happened here and we owe it to all those who didn't survive, help tell their stories. I know this is a concept we can't quite wrap our head around, hell maybe we will never fully understand what happened here or why it did, but I know with all the evil in this world, there more are good people. Kind, loving, beautiful human beings, ones like Peter, that make me have hope in humanity," I finished.

Kowalski stared off into the distance for a moment, the horrific images engraved in his brain, will never leave him, or any of us. He thanked me and descended the steps back to his quarters. I stood at the top of the stairs, looking out over the city towards the trees. This small town sitting just on the edge of the forest, where a darkness was brewing and thriving. If it wasn't for my men stumbling upon that camp, we would never have known it was there, let alone the other three in the area.

The sun was setting, I headed to the mess hall and ate dinner with some of my men before calling it for the night. Tomorrow all 48 German soldiers including SS first commandment officer Himmler will be taken into custody and sent to Britain for further prosecution of their war crimes.

This brought me a sense of relief. And even if these men were put to death, nothing was going to bring back the loved ones they had taken from these survivors, but it was a start.

# Chapter Thirty-Eight
## Aiden

When I entered my room Henry was sitting at my desk, he looked like he had been there for a while, bottle in one hand a glass in the other. He looked tired, drained his eyes red, like he had been crying. I walked over to him softly whispering his name "Henry?" I say. He slowly turned his head toward me; he had a letter open on his desk, the envelope I could see was addressed to him, and next to his was an unopened letter addressed to me. "Henry," I say softly, "Hey, mate you alright?" I asked him. I touched his shoulder gently, removing the glass bottle from his hand. I sat on the edge of the desk facing him, I could see clearly now he had been crying. "What going on mate?" I ask him, looking up at me, the words that came out of his mouth next hit me like a thousand knives were stabbing me in the gut.

"It's…., umm ugh, shit" he said letting out a half laugh, trying not to cry again, "umm it's Abby, she…Jesus," Henry continued." I don't know how to…." he trailed off again.

"It's okay Henry, just take a moment mate, is she hurt?" I asked him.

Trying to calm him down, he finally gathered his composer looked me dead in the eyes and said, "Abby killed herself," he wiped the tears from his face and poured another shot of whiskey in his glass and choked it back. I stood up and stumbled backwards before catching myself.

"Wha…. how what? Whe…when?" I say fumbling the words from my mouth. I was having a hard time trying to form a sentence, my brain was going a thousand miles a minute. "How did this hap…....?" Before I finished my sentence, I caught myself, knowing exactly how this could have happened. Abby had received my letter about Jimmy. "Henry, I'm so sorry, I…." I paused; I didn't know what else to say. "This was all my fault" I said to myself. She is gone because of me.

We sat for hours, not talking just staring off into oblivion.

"This isn't your fault," Henry started, "When I first read the letter,

I was angry, confused and full of rage. I did, at first blame you Aiden. I over came here to scream at you, hell maybe even punch you in the face, but the truth is, none of this is your fault," Henry continued "I know she would be grief-stricken, but I…. I never thought she would have taken her own life. I know Jimmy was her world; her everything, that gentle kind soul of hers, it could not handle losing him," Henry finished.

He took another shot of whiskey, his last, placing both the bottle and glass on the desk. He stood up a little wobbly, "You know I knew something was wrong," he said. I looked at him, slightly confused as to what he had meant by that.

"What do you mean, you could have known? Henry, no one could have known what she was going to do when she found out about Jimmy," I said to Henry. Henry wiping his hands over his face, "The day she took her life, I felt an overwhelming sense of grief rush over me. This feeling of pain, loss, sorrow and then peace. Just peace," he said.

"I brushed it off, thinking it was just a wave of emotions going through me from the loss of Jimmy, but now I know it was her, Abby. It was Abby letting me know she was in immense despair, and now she is at peace," Henry said. He looked over at me, and he embraced me in a hug, "I love you Aiden," Henry said.

"I love you to Henry," I said to Henry, embracing him back.

He walked out the door, heading back to his room to get some rest. I sat down at my desk, I poured myself a tall glass of whiskey, I grabbed the letter addressed to me from Calloway and began to read it.


*Dear Aiden,*

*I'm sorry I didn't write to tell you sooner, but Abby and I had agreed at the time, not to say anything until we felt it was the right moment to do so. With Abby's passing, I feel it is only right to tell you now that Saoirse has been missing for the last Three months. I know what you are thinking, how could I have kept this from you all this time? Honestly, this was one of the hardest things I have ever had to do, but nonetheless it is time to let you know what had happened. So, here it goes.*

*Back in January, Saoirse had joined a group of doctors who routinely travel outside of London's city limits to the countryside, to attend to the medical needs of others out there. She had done this time and time again with no incidents, until her last visit. Saoirse and a group of other nurses were attending to their normal routine visit. Typically, a three day turn around. With the weather being finickity, Abby and I had already planned for Saoirse to return slightly later than normal. When that time though, had come and passed, we had become more worried. We decided to drive out to Sector Six, her hospital sector, maybe with the snowfall their vehicle may have had some trouble.  We weren't expecting anything more than that. But to our dismay, we were proven utterly wrong. When we arrived, we found the first hospital tent, empty, no sign of life, just copious amounts of blood and bodies lying throughout the tent. Saoirse was not amongst those dead in the first tent. After checking all the bodies on the ground and inside the tent for a pulse, they were all dead. We made our way towards the back hospital tent. We could see again, there was no sign of life. Everyone had been killed and still, there was no sign of Saoirse. We searched everywhere for her, called out to her through the woods. Checking every single body over again making sure we didn't miss anything. Leaving no surface untouched. She was just...gone.  Sometime had gone bye and we knew we had done what we could, we decided with a heavy heart it was time to head back to London. We weren't going to find Saoirse out here. Over the course of the last three months, we have gone back several times expanding our search farther into the countryside. Still, there is no trace of her. I do have faith she is still alive; I can still feel her here, and this feeling gives me hope of her return. I won't stop looking for her. Not until she is home.*

*Just know we were not trying to deceive you, with not having informed you sooner.  We were trying to protect you, now I realize that sometimes our own projections on how we feel can muddle the mind and the decisions we choose to make. I hope you can forgive me Aiden; I never meant to hurt you or cause you any turmoil or angst. I was only trying to protect you. I promise you Aiden, I will get Saoirse back. I have not given up hope on her. I hope you will believe me and this gives you some sort of comfort.*

*Sincerely,*
*Calloway*

My mind had so many thoughts, racing through it, my emotions, anger, rage, frustration, sadness, and dread filled my heart. I felt, helpless. While I was furious with Calloway and Abby both for not telling me sooner, I understood their rationalization behind keeping it from me.

Three months ago, we had just defeated the Germans in one of the most brutal and intense battles thus far and I wasn't in the right mindset to have received this news then. If he had told me, then I may have not be here now. I put my head in my hands and cry. I feel like I have failed Saoirse, the love of my life has been taken to God knows where? I stop my mind from thinking about the awful things she is being subjected to. I need to stay positive. She will make it back home to me, safely. I know Calloway won't give up on her and neither will I.

I prayed; I prayed harder than I have ever done before that night. Begging God to bring Saoirse back home safely, to give Henry peace and clarity, and help him overcome his grief, healing his heartache. I prayed to lift Calloway's burdens from him, help him to heal from his feeling of failures with the disappearance of Saoirse and the loss of Abby, neither were his fault, nor could he have prevented or have known what was going to happen. Every night since I had heard of Abby's passing and Saoirse disappearance, I have prayed. I will continue to do so, until Saoirse is back home, and I am home with her. I just hope my prayers will be enough.

# Chapter Thirty-Nine
## Saoirse

Erik Laid out a map of the building and the city limits. He showed me all the military barricades and where we would need to go. He explained how we would slip through beyond these walls, moving through the barricades without them seeing us. "We will leave in the middle of the night; we use the darkness as our cover. We only take those who can walk or run. Anyone else who is unable to do so, we will have to leave behind for now, but we will be back for them." Erik continued, "We cannot risk getting caught. If they catch us, we will be executed, and all of this will be for nothing," he finished.

Taking a moment to process the information, "I can't leave anyone behind," I told him. Erik took in a deep breath, "Listen to me Saoirse, I know you feel like you need to save everyone, but we cannot risk getting caught. I understand the guilt you must feel, I promise you this, if we get caught there is no negotiating, there is no coming back. Just death. I can't even promise your death would be quick or there's. It would be a huge risk bringing anyone incapable of the journey along," Erik Said.

"But what if they kill them because we escaped? Or if they torture them thinking they had any information?" I asked Erik.

"Bottom line is, if we all cannot go then none of us go. Every single woman down there has been tortured, beaten, starved, some have been raped, and you want me to leave the few who are unable to carry themselves through this journey, here alone? Absolutely fucking not" I said firmly staring back at Erik.

Erik knew I was not going to discuss this further. My decision was made, and it was finale. All of us or none of us.

"Okay, we will take everyone, but if any of you falls behind, I cannot and I will not slow down for them! Do you understand me? they will be your responsibility Saoirse," Erik said.

"I know they will, I promise you, we won't slow you down," I said. "Alright, we leave in 3 days. The general will be gone and most of his guard detail will be with him. This will leave gaps and significant amounts of time in between guard changes to allow us to get you all out of here," Erik explained.

"Once I get you through the barricades, I will give you this map here," he shows me a detailed map he has drawn for me, "this map here, it will take you to the boat that I will arrange to take you back to London. You must understand, I cannot continue further on with you, at this point. I will need to get back and return to my post before they suspect anything. Do you understand me?" Erik asked.

"Yes," I said to him.

We get up from the table, "I will give you the map tomorrow evening when I bring you, your food and water," Erik said.

"How will I tell the others?" I asked.

"You don't. The less they know the better it is for them. Only you will know of our plan," Erik said.

"Okay, I understand. What time will you come and get us?" I asked.

"When I open your cell door. I won't know definitively until that evening. You are going have to trust me," Erik said reassuringly.

He was right, I needed to trust him fully or this plan will collapse before we are able to give it a chance. Our lives depend on it.

"We need to mess up your hair a bit and make it look like we....umm, you know," Erik said, his face starting to turn red.

"Yes, okay I can do that," I told him. I ratted my hair, but I know this won't be convincing enough, so I started to smack myself across the face a few times. I need to look like he raped and beat me. Every bit of this needed to be perfect. I wasn't strong enough to leave a big enough bruise on my face.

"Hit me" I asked Erik.

"What?!" Erik in shock, replied.

"Hit me! We need this to be realistic, and I'm not slapping myself hard enough to leave a mark. so hit me," I said to him. He shook his head, "No, Saoirse I can't hit you. I won't hit you," Erik said. I knew then, this man was incapable of hurting me.

"Listen, we need to make this work, I promise you, I will be okay just hit me. Hit me hard enough to leave a mark so it's only the one time," I told him.

"Okay, just the one-time Saoirse," Erik said trembling

Erik raised his hand, hesitating to slap me, I reassured him I was going to be okay and then WHACK!!!! A brutal wave of pain formed across my face. Hot, stinging sensation pained my delicate skin for several moments. I knew we needed a few more smacks like that so I asked him again to smack me, and then one last time. Searing blow to my face one after the other. I made sure to scream loud, crying as hard as I could. Yelling for him to stop hurting me.

"Is that good?" I asked him.

"Yes, that should work," Erik said

Before we walked out, Erik helped me up, gently grabbing me by my arm, "Are you going to be, okay?" He asked me. I gave him an encouraging smile, "Yes, I promise I will be okay," I reassured him. Erik walked me back to my cell throwing me to the ground playing the part as needed. The other soldiers laughed, mocking my cries as they retreated up the stairs. A lump formed in my throat, but I held my composer and swallowed it back down. My face was swollen, tender to the touch. My head was throbbing, so I laid myself down trying to get some sleep. "Three more days," I said to myself, and I will be back home with Abby and Calloway, and this will all seem like a bad nightmare I couldn't wake up from.

# Chapter Forty
## Aiden

*May 3<sup>rd</sup>,1945*

We moved on out from Landsberg and made our way towards Celle. Upon arriving in Celle, we had occupied it rather quickly, and then pushed our way on towards Hamburg. The German flanks were being pushed further back. We had received news that the war in the Pacific was making head way. Looks to be like we will be ending this war sooner than we had thought. April 10$^{th,}$ we moved out of Celle, Germany and arrived in the town of Welle.

We occupied the town in a matter of days, pushing back the last bit of German resistance. We pressed forward into Tostedt on April 18$^{th}$. After the capture of Tostedt, we moved forward through Hollenstedt, we were met with little resistance there. The German soldiers were moving closer to Hamburg gathering all those who were willing, an able to fight. Building up their forces as we pressed on forward, making great headway moving town to town. Nazi civilians were surrendering their towns to us, and any German soldiers who have surrendered, were now POW's, and they would be taken back to London for further prosecution of their war crimes.

On April 20$^{th,}$ the 7$^{th}$ division took Daersternt and Vahrendorf. My squadron stayed here for 5 days gathering all our resources as needed. Refueling our Humvees and tanks, collecting more rifles and ammo, preparing for the battle of Hamburg. We managed to set up a full perimeter around Hamburg blocking in the Germans on all fronts. April 26$^{th,}$ the 12$^{th}$ SS reinforcements regiment who had been mostly made up of those in Hitler's Youth program, some sailors and policemen had waged their attack on our soldiers. Holding their position strongly at first, not allowing us for any further movement, keeping the British forces unable to make headway. The German soldiers and resistance group they had, knew they were blocked in and needed to make their last stand. The fight lasted on through the night. When our British tanks had finally arrived, this allowed for us to apply immense pressure on their line of resistance, causing to push the Germans back into Harburg. 60 of their soldiers dead and over 70 were captured in the end. Overall was a very successful mission.

April 28th, we took Harburg, and on April 29th the German Deputation for the city had surrendered. May 1st German general Alwin Wolzes, appeared in his staffs car waving a white flag, he surrenders upon hearing the news that Berlin had been taken by the Soviets on April 30th. Hitler had committed suicide in his bunker, the coward took his own life, rather than face the wrath for his war crimes. What a disgrace that man was, diabolical. The news rang out, and the German Flanks had begun to surrender. By May 3rd the war had finally come to an end in Europe. Now, we finally could feel a sense of relief. The cheers rang out through Harburg as we all celebrated in unison.

I stood next to Henry, watching as our men drank and ate on long throughout the night. The sound of freedom ringing in the air for those of us lucky to had survived the war. For those who perished, our fallen brothers in arms, we toasted to their memory and their ultimate sacrifice for their country. My mind, in midst of all the celebrating was finding it hard to focus on the good knows, knowing my darling Saoirse was still out there somewhere. My feeling of eagerness to return home was papabile. "Sir" I looked to my left, a solider had a letter in his hand holding it out to me.

I had hesitated to take it, giving the last letter I and Henry both had received was nothing sort of despair, I took a moment, before I was able to grab it from his hand, Henry took it upon himself to grab it first; then thanking the soldier as he turned and walked off.

"You want me to open it?" Henry asked.

"No, No mate that's alright," I said to him, my body riddled with anxiety.

I stared blankly, lost in my thoughts before returning to the present. "I'm going to find a quiet spot to read this," I said to Henry.

"Okay, are you sure you will be, okay? I can come sit with you!" Henry said.

"No mate, really, I will be alright. I just think I need to read this one on my own," I said to him. Waving Henry on to go join the others, I walked off and found a spot, on a corner of the city in between two buildings, quite enough and private enough for me. I pulled the letter out of my pocket. Twirling it in my fingers, trying to gain the strength to open it up. Every time I tried, I kept failing, tears welling in my eyes, I couldn't help but think of the worst possible piece of information that has been written within this letter. I took in a deep breath once more, then started to unfold the letter. I wiped the tears from my face, exhaling all the air from my body, turned the letter over and read the first couple of words.

*Dear Aiden......*

# Chapter Forty-One
## Saoirse

Three days. That's how long I need to hold it all together. We are nearly there, nearly home. Erik is coming tonight to give me the map, for us to make our way out of the city walls and back to the boat that will be taking us home, to London. My fears, and worries have been a constant voice in my head. I try and quite them down rather quickly. There is no room for any negative thoughts, not here, not now.

That evening Erik brought me my dinner like he said he would be doing. A half cup of water and a small bowl of slop. Just enough to keep us alive, but not enough for any nourishment. All of us are plain skin and bones, starving slowly to death. What an awful way to go. I would rather they beat me to death, than die here of starvation. When Erik entered my cell, he handed me my tray as normal. The map was located under it, taped to the bottom. When Erik had left, with a mindful haste, I gentle removed the map from the bottom of the tray and hid it, in a chiseled-out hole that I had carved out in the wall here behind my cot. Not visible to the naked eye.

After our "dinner" Erik returned for the empty contents, he handed them off to the other soldier and ordered him to take it back up to the kitchen. Erik would be on Guard duty tonight, which would allow me to look over the map intensely. All night long, I kept repeating the names I had read. Imagining where we were and where we needed to go. I studied the map repeatedly, until it was seared into my brain. When I felt confident enough with the map, I ripped it up and placed it within the wall. The evening before our planned escape, I couldn't help but think about Calloway and Abby. I know they have been waiting for my return. Never giving up hope I would make it back to them alive. And then there's Aiden, oh my sweet Aiden. I'm sure he has been made aware of my kidnapping by now. But what if he thinks I'm dead? I have been here for so long, even I would have slight doubts of mu survival if I was them. My thoughts start to trail off into a pit of darkness and before I go any deeper, I pull them back into the light again. "Stop it Saoirse!" I say to myself. "Aiden knows you are alive, and you will be in each other's arms soon," I said to myself. My mind thinks of a time when we will all be together again, just as before. The six of us living together happily, no cares or worries in the world. My heart beating more calmly as I think of Aiden. One more night, and I will be home. I took in a deep breath, then let it all out, I needed to get some rest. My body will need all the negeri I can muster up for this journey, and so I roll to my side and try to get some shut eye.

First morning light I was up. I could see the small light beaming from the tiny window above my prison cell, I awoke and sat straight up looking around. The night guard who had switched mid shift with Erik was not standing at my cell door. An eerie silence sent chills through my bones. A feeling I didn't like at all. "Something was wrong, it's never this quiet and there is never not a guard on duty," I thought to myself. I stand up and walk over to the cell door, peering through the bars down the corridor. I could only see so far, and from the looks of it, no one was there. Forced to be quite and not call out to anyone, if someone is there then I will reap the consequences. But I needed to know. "Hello" I yelled out down the corridor. Nothing, but my voice reverberating off the brick walls came back to me.

"Hello? Is anyone there?" I yelled out again. Still nothing.

I felt the pit in my stomach start to turn. The other young women came over to their cell doors, waiting to hear anyone coming down the steps.

"You shouldn't be calling out Saoirse." Becca said.

"I know Becca, but the guard is not here, and it is quiet, too quiet something isn't right," I replied to her.

"What do you think happened?" Marjorie asked.

"I don't know, this could either be a good thing or a very bad thing," I said cautiously back to Marjorie.

"Maybe the war has come to end, and we have finally won?" Becca stated, with confusion and hopefulness in her tone. My heart quickened at the thought of freedom and to the end of our prison days. "If, hypothetically, the war has ended and they all fled, we are still locked down here until someone comes and finds us," I thought. That's even if "They" whoever they are, knows we are down here and will come looking for us. "Think Saoirse, think! I say softly.

"What about Erik? He must come back here, there is no way he would have abandon us down here," I said to myself.

Panic is setting in, I feel it in my chest, get tighter, the air leaving my lungs but not filling them back up. "Slow down Saoirse" I said to myself, "Everything is going to be okay. Breath in and Breath out. There you go, in and out." Calming myself down.

"Now let's keep calm and try to figure this out." Finishing my thought.

"Alright, ladies listen, there is a possibility something big has happened and the Soldiers have all left," I said. I can hear the women begin to panic, voices growing louder, their cries of desperation echoing their chambers.

"What do you mean they have left?" one woman said.

"If they have left, then that means no one is going to find us!" Another one replied.

They all started to speak over each other, their voices growing louder, "QUIET!" I screamed out. The room fell silent. "Listen to me" I started, "I know this is scary, I know there are a million thoughts running through your mind, I too am scared, but I promise you someone is going to come back and get us. Alright?" I said to them. "Ho…… How do you know?" Anna asked in between her cries, "Because a few nights ago I met a man named Erik when I was taken to his soldier quarters," I continued, "he promised me he would get us all out of here. I say to them.

"What if he was lying?" one of the women yelled.

"You just trusted him? He is a SS Nazi Soldier. What if he had planned this and you fell for his schemes and now, we are stuck here and left to die!" The women finished.

"What's your name?" I asked her.

" "My name is Marissa," she replied.

"Marissa, I know this is scary and I understand why you would think that, but this man Erik, instead of beating me or raping me or even killing me like he could have; he trusted me and told me who he was," I continued "Erik is a Russian spy. He and I hatched up a plan to help us escape and get us out safely, back home to London," I told them.

"And you believed him?" Marissa replied.

"Yes…. yes, I did, and I still do, there was something about him, he felt sincere, and I trust, no I believe, he will be coming back for us. I promise you all. Erik will come for us. Erik was going to come and get us out tonight, all of us. He gave me a map of the city, and he has a boat waiting to take us back to England," I said.

"Why didn't you tell us this?" Becca asked.

"Because Erik, Both, Erik and I agreed the less you all knew the safer you were," I replied.

Their voices and cries were beginning to settle. I knew it wouldn't be for long. By night fall, there is no stopping them from being hysterical if Erik doesn't show. I would be made not only a fool, but and ignorant woman who was nothing short of desperate to save her friends. I prayed that day harder than I had before. Begging, pleading with God to spare our souls and bring us home. Evening had begun to fall upon us and Erik was still not here.

My tears fell silently out my eyes and down my face, realizing this may be the way, I die, the way we all die. Starved and abandon in a prison cell. Believing in the wrong person who I thought was my friend. Who will find my body? Who would tell Aiden of what has happened to me. My heart was breaking at the thought of Aiden's pain mourning over me. He would never recover; I know I wouldn't if I had ever lost him.

Suddenly, the door on top of the steps flew open, I bolted up and ran to my cell door to see who was coming down the steps. My heart pounding violently in my chest, the anxiety rising, as my skin began to feel hot. I see a man, Erik I thought, unable to see his face clearly. I smile hoping it is him, as the man draws closer his image is not that of Erik's, but of the General who I had met at the hospital, the first encounter many months ago. The general who had killed many of my friends and all those poor people before kidnapping me and a few others, holding us all hostage.

I backed up away from the cell door, he stood there in front of the door, glaring at me, his cold, icy blue eyes peering into my soul. This man had soulless eyes. When he looks at you, you can't help but get shivers up your spine. He smiles at me, his teeth glowing yellow, his sinister smirk sitting across his pocked scarred face. He opens the door and I think "maybe I can run? Just move your feet Saoirse. Don't just stand there! Move your fucking feet," I said under my breathe. He rushes toward me and I jolt to the left, catching him off guard but before I make it to the cell door he jumps at me catching my feet and tripping me, causing me to lose my balance and fall to the floor. "LET ME GO!" I scream at him, as he starts to drag my body back towards him. "GET THE FUCK OFF OF ME!" I scream. I can hear the other girls screaming for help hoping someone will hear their cries.

He finally has me under him. His body sitting on my waistline. I'm unable to move out from under him, for his body strength is much stronger than mine. He grabbed my arms and puts them both up above my head, interlocking them in one of his hands. "NO! NO! PLEASE STOP!" I pleaded with him "YOU DON'T HAVE TO DO THIS!" I screamed at him. He's unbuttoning his pants, grinning at me, lusting over how fearful he has made me.  He takes his free hand and runs it across my face over my lips pressing his thumb towards my mouth. "Bite it Saoirse bite it hard!" I think to myself. I wait for his thumb to slide further into my mouth. I calm myself making him think I have giving up and he has won. He shoves his thumb just a bit further in, "NOW!" My inner voice screams, I bite down as hard as I could. I can taste the iron in my mouth, I heard his screams. I let go of his thumb, blood dripping down the side of mouth, I'm spitting it out, not wanting to swallow any of his blood. He placed his thumb to his chest, a hard smack is heard as his hand made its way across my face, letting go of my arms. Blood once again, pools in my mouth, my face burning from the sting of the slap. "YOU STUPID FUCKING CUNT!" he screamed out. "YOU BIT MY FUCKING THUMB OFF! YOU DIRTY WHORE!" He screamed at me.

With my arms free, I quickly think of how I can get out from under him. He is still focused on his wound; this gives me a brief few seconds to think and think fast. I am not free yet. I look around seeing if there is anything I reach I can grab. I don't see anything I can use; I'm feeling myself beginning to panic, that's when I see his pistol on his hip. I reach to grab it pulling it from his belt, this all feeling like I was moving in slow motion, his eyes grew wide, looking down at his belt then back down at me. I pull the slide back releasing the bullet into the chamber, aimed for in between his eyes and pulled the trigger. "BANG!" The gun goes off and for a second, I thought I had missed. Then I refocus my vision, and see the hole in between his eyes, blood draining from it, as he falls off me, onto his side. I let out a feral scream, gasping for air, like I had been holding my breath this entire time. I heard more footsteps coming down the stairs. I push myself out from underneath of him. Blood stained my mouth and clothes.

I stand up, my head woozy from the hard hit he gave me, I stumble just a bit. When I find my balance, I look up, and Erik is standing in front of my cell door. "I knew you would come back for us," I said in a half smile. I go to walk towards him wobbly still almost collapsing, but not before Erik runs towards me and grabbed a hold of me. He looks me over, then looks at the dead general on the floor. "Don't worry he got it much worse than I did!" I said with smile, putting my arm around Erik's neck. He uses his other arm placing it around my waist to hoist me up. He ordered his men to unlock the other cell doors and bring the other women upstairs.

We made our way outside, "What Happened? Where did everyone go?" I asked him.

"Hitler killed himself, we took Berlin, and all the SS soldiers, the German Army has begun to flee from the city," he continued, "The war is over Saoirse, you are going home now," he said. I pause to turn to him, "Thank you Erik," I said to him with tears filling my eyes. "Come on, let's get you back home," he said softly, with a smile.

They loaded us up into a few cars and drove us over to the dock. They gave us all a new set of clothes, cleaned our wounds and gave us some food and water. "Well, this is goodbye my friend," Erik said. "Thank you, thank you for coming back for us and keeping your word," I said to him. He tipped his hat, smiling back at me and started to walk away, "Erik!" I called out once more to him. He turned around and before he could say anything, I embraced him in a hug.

"I hope to see you again soon. Aiden would love to meet you, my friend who risked his life to save us," I said to Erik.
"I would love to meet him one day Saoirse, it would be my honor," Erik said, hugging me one last time before helping me onto the boat. I stood at the bow, watching Erik and all of Germany disappear into the distance.

I let out a sob, my breath shaky as the fresh salty air stung the wounds on my face. The summers sun warming my face as I turned it up towards the sun. Becca, Marjorie, Marissa and Anna, join me on the bow, holding one another close, and tightly, for the first time in months. I leaned my head against Becca's, "We are finally going home," I said to her. She gives me a smile, both of us looking out into the horizon, our battles are not quite over just yet, now the healing has begun to start. We, the 5 of us, have a bond unbroken by evil tyrants, and we will all remember the strength we gave to one another, in desperate times of survival, these women, my sisters, we have survived, we are finally free, and we are finally going home.

# Chapter Forty-Two
### Aiden

*My Darling Aiden,*

*I wanted to write and let you know I am home, and I am safe. Although my feelings are quite joyful to be back, I am also grief stricken to hear of the passing of both our sweet Abby and Jimmy. My heart has been crippled with the pain and loss of two souls we have loved and had the pleasure of being loved by in our lives. My hope is they have been reunited in another life and are now at peace.*

*A lot has happened, the things…. the things I and the other girls had been through, are words I am not ready to say out loud. I promise in time I will tell you everything. Just know my love, I am doing well, and I am anxiously waiting for your return home. Many thoughts of you, is what kept me alive, and gave me the strength to fight hard, to return home to you.*

*Aiden my darling love, I love you, I long await until I am in your arms again.*

*Love eternally,*
*Saoirse*

I read the letter once more, then again to make sure the words, I was reading were true. Saoirse my beloved, was home and safe, waiting for me to return to her. I sobbed uncontrollably at the mere thought of having almost lost her, and now that she is home, my heart aches for her. Abby is gone, her best friend, her sister, and to have to mourn her alone despairing. I read the letter one finale time before folding it up and placing it back into my jacket pocket. I wiped my face and went to look for Henry, to tell him the good news.

The men were still cheering, drinking bottles of wine, whiskey, and beer alike. The town folk had fixed up all the food they could muster in celebration of the wars end, and all I could think about was

Saoirse.

I found Henry celebrating with some of our friends.

"Hey mate, can I borrow you for a sec?" I asked Henry.

"Yeah, of course mate," Henry replied. We walked over to a corner wall, just far enough away from the other soldiers. I could tell he was nervous, fearing bad news no doubt.

"Is everything okay?" Henry asked me.

"Umm…I wanted to let you know, Saoirse, She…." I was chocking up at the thought of saying the words out loud.

"It's alright mate take your time," Henry said to me.

Pausing for a moment, I look up and smile at Henry, "Saoirse is home Henry. She is finally home, and she is safe. That's what the letter was telling me. it was from her," I said to Henry trying to fight back more tears.

'Wha…. that's exciting news mate!" Henry exclaimed, embracing me in a hug.

"That's incredible, wow, thank god she has made it home," Henry said.

"Did she tell you of anything that had happened?" Henry asked.

"No, she isn't quite ready to talk about it, I doubt she wants to tell me in a letter either. A part of me doesn't want to know what happened to her. The other part wants to find out so I can kill every Fucking bloke that laid a hand on her," I said.

"Yeah, that's understandable, I would do the same for Calloway," Henry said.  Both of us feeling a mix of happiness and sadness for the news of Saoirse's return home.

"I just want to be home with her now," I said to Henry.

"You will soon enough, and once you do, you will never let her out of your sight again," Henry chuckles.

"You are absolutely right about that, I will never leave her again, ever," I said somberly to Henry.

"Come on, let's go celebrate the good news," Henry said to me. We walk back toward the crowd; Henry grabbed a bottle of whiskey and 2 glasses, pouring us a tall one and said a toast.

"To Saoirse, I know she has been through it, when I get back to her, so I can help her heal. To Abby and Jimmy, and their forever eternal peace. I hope they are finally at rest and are happy together. To All our brothers we have lost, may they never be forgotten, and may their souls find the will to rest easy. To you, Henry, for being the best mate and brother I could ever have. You have helped me survive in this war. Kept me alive, to return home to Saoirse. Your strength is unparalleled mate, and I thank you for that," I continued, "Finally, to the rest of us, the living. May we heal from these horrors and all that we have seen. May the world be gentle and kind so we can heal and prosper in this life. May we forgive ourselves for the losses, the ones we couldn't save, may they forgive us, and their souls rest leave this earth and find serenity in death," I said, picking up the glass and tossing it back, the burning sensation, moving down my throat, warming my body as it hits my stomach.

"Here, here," Henry said, tossing his shot back. Clearing his throat Henry starts his toast.

"To Calloway, for our future and the wonderful things we will accomplish, to Saoirse and you, Aiden, your future children and for finding prosperity and comfort as we all live out the rest of days. Lastly, to our parents, who had lost their lives and even though they are no longer with us, we have felt their presence all around us, guiding us and protecting us through this hell hole. May they find peace and serenity as well," Henry said, both toss back another shot of whiskey.

"Alright mate, that's enough celebrating for me, I'm going to head back and get some shut eye," I said to Henry.

"Yeah, same here mate, hopefully we can rest easy tonight," Henry said.

"Me too," I replied. We hugged each other then retreated to our rooms. Instantly, when I made my way through the door I fell straight down on my stomach, onto the bed. Rolling over on to my back, my thoughts slipped into memories of Saoirse and me. And for the first time in 6 years, I fell asleep with ease, for the first time since the war had begun.

# Chapter Forty-Three
## Homecoming

The War in Europe ended on May 7th, 1945. Several months later in August, we had dropped two atomic bombs on Japan, causing for their final surrender. Thus, ending the war officially on September 2nd, 1945. Henry and I were able to return home in June of 1945. We both received the Purple heart for our bravery and valiant sacrifices, of those we had saved in the battle with the Nazi regime before we had landed in Celle, Germany. Out manned and out gunned, we still had managed to break down their defenses. Jeremy had received a purple heart for his heroism. His selfless act saved countless soldiers' lives that day.

Henry and I boarded a boat that transported us from Austria Back to London. I stood out on the bow the day we were set to make landfall. My bag ready to go, I could not contain my excitement. Being away from Saoirse for 6 years was entirely far too long and it was something I never wanted to repeat again as long as I live. Henry came up from behind, putting me in a playful head lock. The two of us smiling ear to ear as we eagerly waited for our docking.

"What if she doesn't recognize me, Henry?" I asked.

"Aiden, when two souls like yours and Saoirse, are gone for long periods of time; when they finally meet again, the memories they have shared, is reignited when brought together again," Henry continued, looking at me, then looking out into the ocean, "this war. It has changed us all, but where there is love, compassion and patience, there is understanding and acceptance. A chance to grow and heal. It won't be easy adjusting from what we have all been through. We have each other, and we have unconditional love for one another, with all those things combined, we will be just fine. I promise," Henry finished.

"You are right Henry, I guess it's just first-time jitters from having been gone for so long," I said to him.
"I know, I feel the same way mate. Everything is going to be okay. You will see," Henry said.

We stared off into the open sea. I know what he was saying was true. Saoirse and I, once back in each other's arms again, will have felt like no time has passed.

The boat was finally making its approach towards the dock. Henry and I stood by waiting for the bridge to lower. All of us filed into a line, as several of us soldiers were making our way down the bridge and on to the dock. My boots, having not touched the sea worn wood in years, gave me a sense of comfort, familiarity. I started searching the crowd for Saoirse's face. So many unfamiliar faces surrounded me, Henry and I were making our way through the countless people in the crowds searching for their loved ones as well.

"You see them mate?" I asked Henry.

"No, not yet," Henry replied.

We kept on walking straight down the docks, my nerves started to take hold, and my hands were beginning to clam up. What if she changed her mind? What if this was all too much for her? The time away, what had happened to her. Maybe she blames me now for Abby's death. All these thoughts came rushing through my mind, like a freight train. I'm working myself up, as I start to calm my mind down again, Henry's hand touches my shoulder. I pause and stop walking; I look over at him "what?" I asked. Henry, grinning ear to ear, "Look over their mate!" Henry smiles, nudging his head in a forward direction.

I looked straight out, just at the end of the pier there she stood. Beautiful, radiant just as I remembered her. I was frozen for a split second; slight bit of fear came over me. Then she caught my gaze, our eyes meeting again for the first time in years. Saoirse, smiling from ear to ear, she starts to make her way towards me. The dock was crowded as we pushed our way through the people, moving faster than before. "Excuse me sir. I'm sorry ma'am," I said, as we were getting closer.

"Aiden!" I heard her call out.

"Saoirse!" I replied. Suddenly, I lost sight of her. I'm spinning around in circles, frantically moving my eyes through the many faces of people around me.

"Saoirse! Saoirse wher…" I yelled out, when just there a few feet from me, she was standing. I dropped my bag, and she leapt into my arms. Holding on to her tightly, I set her feet back down on the dock, putting her face in my hands.

"Hello my love," I said to her. Gosh her smile and those eyes, she brushed back my hair from my face, "Hello Darling," she said to me as I moved her face closer to mine and begin to gently kiss her soft lips.

I couldn't let go of her, not just yet. We stood amongst the crowd of people passing by just holding onto one another. Henry, Calloway, and Saoirse and I, our family was finally together again.

"Oh Aiden, you are…. you are as how I remembered you. You haven't changed a bit," Saoirse said.

"I feel much older," I jokingly replied. She smiled at me tears of joy in her eyes.

"Come on you two let's get you both home we have loads to celebrate and tons of food to eat," Calloway said.

We headed back to the house; London had seemed to be recovering rather well. When we made it back to the house Henry and I set our bags in our bedrooms. Everything still looked the same, the smell, the pictures on the wall, it was all as I had remembered it to be. I changed out of my dressings and put something more casual and comfortable on. We gathered around the dining table, sitting here with this beautiful dinner, and just across from Saoirse and I, two chairs sat empty. The feeling of Abby and Jimmy's absent presence was felt deeply.

"They should be here" Saoirse said. I took her hand in mine rubbing my fingers across her soft skin.

"I know love," I said softly to her. Clearing my throat of the lump that was forming, I stood up and made a toast.

"To our safe return home, to love, hope and new beginnings. To those we miss dearly, they may be gone, but they will never be forgotten, and to our future's may they be everlasting and bright," I said holding a glass of champagne, raising our glasses high, taking a sip.

Dinner was remarkable. We finished our meals and washed up for the night, all of us tired and ready for bed. Saoirse and I made passionate love that night. As if no time had gone by at all, our two souls, remembering each other's touch and falling back into rhythm naturally. Unable to let go of each other we made love all night long well into the early morning. When we did come up for air, Saoirse laid her head on my chest, stroking her soft skin, listening to her breathing in and breathing out. She was safe and asleep, and I thought to myself "I am finally home."

# Chapter Forty-Four
Our New Beginnings

The months passed us by. Some days being harder than others when it came to adjusting back to our "normal" routines again. Nightmares kept me up most nights, in the beginning. Aiden had his own demons he was fighting as well. I found it hard in the beginning to talk about what had happened. We both did. We comforted each other and allowed for us both to find the will to communicate the horrors we had experienced we were both ready. A long time had gone by, and when I felt I was healed enough, I was able to sit down with Aiden, and in great detail, explain the atrocities I and the other woman had been through. Aiden, sat quietly as I went over every count of tragedy. When I was done, he held me in his arms, comforting me as I cried. Unable to do so before, now that I had my person home, my safety net, I was able to fully give myself to him and let go of all my burdens, grief and heartache. Aiden had done the same, now both feeling more free from the pain, we could heal together, now that we have healed separately.

We all agreed it would be in our best interest to move from the city, out of our flat and out to the countryside. All of us in need of a fresh start, Aiden and I would move into my parents' house and Calloway and Henry would move into a small cottage just down the road from us. I quickly became pregnant with our first child after Aiden had returned home. We had made a few trips out there to the farm, making sure everything was in good standing condition. Which to our surprise, it was mostly untouched. Minor fixings here and there, and more than ready for living souls to be in it once again.

Come packing day, there wasn't too much of our belongings to pack up. It was rather easy going. After we finished with our bedroom we moved on into Abby and Jimmy's room. None of us had been in their room since we have been home. Calloway couldn't bring himself to go in their room. He is still haunted, by the memory from finding Abby that dreadful day.

I took a deep breath in and let it out slowly. I turn the knob, slowly opening her door. Their room, it's as if their life, had been frozen in time. Her drapes were open, with the sunlight casting a perfect ray of light over her bed. Her nightstand was covered with dust, on there stood a picture of her and Jimmy, it had been taken by Calloway on our wedding night. Right after Jimmy had proposed. The smiles on their faces, you can feel their love radiating through the picture.

Grabbing the picture from the desk, analyzing it more closely. I rub my fingers over the picture, "I miss you Abby" I say to myself. I hug the picture frame to my chest, then place it next to me on the bed. Next, I grab the small stack of books, Jane Austin, Charles Dickens, a few others, amongst them was her diary. I wipe the dust off each book, including her diary and set them aside. I open her drawer to her nightstand and find a picture of her and I as kids. Making goofy faces, Abby always had a way of making me laugh. Sometimes, she made me laugh so hard that my stomach would ache afterwards. I smile at the thought of this memory, before moving on and pulling out a few more photos of her and I, a few of her and Henry as kids and a couple more of her and Jimmy. I place them all on the bed neatly. One last photo laid tucked in the back of the drawer. I leaned in and pulled it out, it was a picture of her parents on their wedding night. I rub my finger gentle over it removing the silt, "I hope you are with them now," I saw to myself, putting their picture with the others.

I move from corner to corner of her entire room combing over every last trace of her. Tears were falling from my face as I started to pack everything into boxes. Aiden had come in and was gathering all of Jimmy's belongings, placing them alongside Abby's things, when the boxes were full, we folded them up, taped them shut, and labeled them "Abby and Jimmy's memories" I handed it to Aiden to take down to the car. Before walking out and forever closing the door on this chapter, I scanned her room one last time. Memories coming to life as if I was watching it on a movie reel. So many beautiful moments we had shared together throughout our lives. I stood there just a moment longer, when Aiden came up behind me. "Are you okay?" He asked me.

"Yes, I'm okay love, just taking a moment before I close this chapter of our lives," I said to Aiden.

"Take all the time you need love; we can stay as long as you need to" Aiden said. I took his hand in mine, grateful I have him here by my side.

"No, it's okay. I'm ready to go," I whispered softly.

"Okay, Darling," he said, kissing the back of my head. I go to close the door and a cool breeze brush by me. I look towards the window, thinking I had left it open; but it was closed. I feel my hair move slightly, a joyful feeling passes through me, I knew then it was Abby, she was here with me letting me know it's okay. She is happy and at peace. "I feel you sweet Abby," I whispered softly under my breath. I feel the soft air pass by me once more, closing door behind me, ending a chapter of my life, making room for new beginnings.

*Saoirse's Poem*

*August 1946.*

### *Grief*

*Grief, it has no mercy, for it is a constant reminder of what we have lost. It's forever boding in its form and while it has no intention on being malice, it presents itself as such. Grief is all the love you didn't get to give, It's the wishing you had "more time," and the "what if's" that run through your mind. It's the replays of moments together. The "how could I have not seen their pain," to the "they were my responsibility." Grief, while making us feel soulless, it is a hefty reminder that we are human; through grief we feel our heart shatter into a million pieces, the feeling of un-ableness to get up out of bed, to simple tasked around the house or simply, pick up the pieces of the life that has been left to you. Forcing you to find a way to bring it back together again, as if it will be the same, when we both know it won't be. Grief has no time, no end date to healing. I wish time was more kind to you sweet Abby. Wild like the wildflowers and free as the wind ever flowing through our hair. You had a smile that lit up every room you walked in. Abby was as beautiful, as the sun's rays shinning down on a warm summers night. Jimmy was Abby's Eden. Two souls forever intertwined in life and in death. Forever Eternal Soulmates. Even though you are no longer here, I wish you could see how happy we are, but for now, I will look to the sky and tell it to the stars, in hopes you will hear me. Rest in serenity our Dearest Abby.*

# Chapter Forty-Five
Closure

A few years had passed by since we left our apartment. Aiden had begun working as an investor, he helped Calloway opened an art gallery. Calloway's finest pieces were displayed for the world to see. We had gotten pregnant with our first child, in August of 1945. A little girl, we named Abigail Rae Palo, Abby for short. Shortly soon after, just before Abby's first birthday we found out we were pregnant with twin Boys. Calvin James Palo and Calloway Armise Palo. Then our last sweet child, little Grace-Lynn Charlotte Palo, arrived 2 years after the twin boys.

Our family was full and complete. I had decided that I wanted to be at home with our babies. I had left the nursing field after we had Abby. It was an easier decision than I thought it would be. I had a hard time adjusting, after everything that had happened, it was incredibly hard to focus and do my work. The hospital wasn't the same without Abby, everything I had seen and been through, I just wanted quietness and a sense of calming in my life, in our life. When Abigail arrived, she had solidified my feelings even more. The day Abby was born, started off with a heavy rainstorm. Was freezing outside, the wind had picked up rapidly, we were worried we might lose power. I was at home, in the comfort of our bedroom. I labored all through the day and night. The storm was raging, it helped keep my mind off the pain. Our doctor, Dr. Connelly, was making sure my breathing was steady and controlled.

"Okay, Mrs. Palo, it's time to push," Dr. Connelly said.

"Mmm…. I can't, I can't do it! I'm so tired," I cried out.

"I know Mrs. Palo, but your baby is ready to come out now," Dr. Connelly assured me.

"It hurts, I ca…" I said catching my breath. Aiden was holding my hand, stroking my hair back from my face. He leaned down kissing my forehead, "You can do this Saoirse, you are strong my love. Stronger than anyone here," Aiden said to me.

I look over at him, sweat beading from my face.

"Aiden, it hurts, I… I don't know if I am strong enough," I said quietly, getting ready to cry. He got down on his knees, looking me in my eyes, "you can do this my love. I am right here next to you. If you need to scream, then scream. But you must push my love," Aiden said.

I took in another deep breath and let it on out.

"Okay, I can do this, I'm ready!" I say to Aiden and Dr. Connelly.

"That's right Mrs. Palo, on the count of three you are going to give me a big push," Dr. Connelly said

"ONE! TWO! THREE! PUSH!!" Dr. Connelly encouraged Saoirse to push.

"AWWWW!" I scream out as I give all my energy to push.

"You are doing great love," I heard Aiden say.

"Okay, Mrs. Palo, I can see the head, come on and give me another push," Dr. Connelly said.

I breathe in again and when I breathe out I give one hard push.

"Okay, the shoulders are out, Mrs. Palo, one last and final push you can do this," Dr. Connelly said.

"You can do this Saoirse" I heard Aiden say again. I squeezed his hand hard, harder than I have before. I let out a loud blood curdling scream, and then I heard a baby's cries. Our sweet little baby's cries.

"It's a girl" Dr. Connelly said holding her up for me to see.

He placed our baby on my chest, putting a blanket over the two of us. I could feel Aiden kissing my face, moving my face to meet his lips with mine.

"You did remarkable, darling," Aiden said to me. Dr. Connelly made sure I okay before heading on home. Our house was so quiet, the three of us, in our bed. Aiden and I couldn't take our eyes off her.

"Have you picked out a name, my darling" Aiden asked. I looked up at him, then back at our baby.

"I want to name her Abigale, Abigail Rae Palo," I said to him.

Aiden kisses me on the head, "I think that is a beautiful name," He said to me.

"Hello, Abigail, I'm your mum and this is your dad," I said, kissing her head gently, her big green eyes staring back into mine. I thought my heart was going to explode. The love I had for her, for all my children. Each one making their arrival into the world. Our heart's expanded that much more. The love we felt for them was unlike anything before. A love so deep, and unconditional. We would do everything in our power to protect them and keep them safe.

# Chapter Forty-Six
## Us

Calloway and Henry made a beautiful life for themselves. They bought a cute cottage just down the road from us. A mini farm they had full of cows, goats, chickens, and with a beautiful garden. Calloway had his studio; it had become very successful. He held expos, several of his paintings had become known around the world. Henry finished earning his degree, becoming a professor of history, and was hired on to teach at Cambridge University. They both built a beautiful, wonderful life together.

That goes without saying that the war had taken its toll on them both, Henry at the age of 40 was diagnosed with a brain tumor. They gave him 3 months to live, he ended up living another 3 years. He passed away with Calloway by his side at the age of 43. Calloway was never the same after Henry's passing, losing someone you love, watching them slowly dwindle away, and not being able to help them. It was painful, brought back so many memories for Calloway, the helplessness he had felt during the war. Unable to save those around him. When Henry got sick, those memories were drudged up from the grave. Henry, being the sweet soul that he was, never lost his spirits. He always remained positive, even when he was on his death bed. His funeral was beautiful. We held it in their backyard. Henry wanted to be cremated and have his ashes spread throughout their flower garden. Calloway had made a beautiful headstone for Henry, marking his grace, we all stood surrounding one another, sharing beautiful memories before letting Henry's ashes go. I checked in on Calloway daily, I know he was grief-stricken. Calloway had let his art fall to the wayside. He closed his art studio, became quite the recluse. I would spend many hours with Calloway, trying to cheer him up, focus on the positive things in life. Some days were better than others. I didn't blame him though. If I had lost Aiden, my world would have been shattered. Having my children to live on for would be the only reason for me to continue living.

Calloway and Henry, only had each other.

A few months later, we had received the devastating news that Calloway, at the age of 45, was diagnosed with leukemia. A short year later, Calloway had passed away in the comfort of his and Henry's home surrounded by Aiden, Myself and our four kids. He was ready to go. He didn't want any treatment, he just waited for his time to come, to be reunited with Henry again. He would often tell me that he saw Henry everywhere, in his dreams, out by the garden, talking with him, telling him they would be together soon. At first, I thought it was the cancer taking its toll, but then again, I think when it comes to our time, the loved ones we have lost come back to help ease us into the next life. When Calloway had passed, he too wished to be cremated and to have his ashes spread throughout their garden, just like we did for Henry. Calloway had arranged for a beautiful headstone to be placed next to Henry's. They had left their house to Aiden and me. To do what we pleased with it. We took great care of it over the years. Never allowing for it to fall to pieces.

When Abby had grown and gone to school for nursing, during her studies she had met her now husband there. He was going to school to be a doctor. Luke was his name. Those two were smitten with each other. They reminded me of Aiden and myself, so young, so full of love. After they had gotten married, Aiden and I, with Abby being the oldest and the first to be married. We had gifted her uncle's cottage to the two of them as a wedding gift. In hopes of making, it their own, they went on to have two little girls. Grace-Lynn after her little sister, and Saoirse Rae, after me. Oh, what bright young girls they were. The first set of grandbabies to be born. Aiden and I were over the moon. As the years pressed on, our twin boys Calloway and Calvin, Calloway followed in his Uncle Henry's footsteps and became a professor. He taught poetry and literature, he too, taught at Cambridge. Calloway went on to marry a young lady by the name of Susan. They had 5 kids together. They traveled the world, finally settling down in Yorkshire. We visited them often. Calvin Joined the Air Force, becoming a pilot. He was soon brought on by the British embassy, to serve as an ambassador. Calvin was a part of supporting diplomatic relations with the United States of America during the Vietnam war. He met his wife Roslyn, while he was stationed in Spain. Roslyn was a teacher from Wales. She moved back home to Spain, after there was a shortage of teachers there. When they had married, because he would be stationed all over, she was able to teach kids in every country they were stationed. She was an incredible woman; all our kids spouses were remarkable. Calvin and Roslyn went on to have five beautiful children, When Calvin retired, they were able to settle down here, just outside the city limits of London.

Our daughter Grace-Lynn had fallen ill when she was only 4 years old. She had contracted Polio. At the time, she had not received the vaccine, by the time we were able to have done so, it was too late. The disease, as vile and debilitating as it was, in the end, it had taken her life. Our world was once again met with great devastation. There is nothing like the death of your child, no parent should have to bury their baby. We laid her to rest in our garden next to her aunt Abby and uncle Jimmy's graves. Two crosses we had made in place for the two of them even though we did not have their bodies, we wanted a burial garden for those we have lost to keep close to us. Abby, Jimmy, My parents, Aiden's parents and now our sweet Grace-Lynn.

Through the fires of war, the death of our friends, bringing new life into the world, our kids, to the death of Henry and Calloway, and then loss of our little girl; Aiden and I have overcome every emotional barrier thrown at us and we have never been stronger. Aiden is my best friend, the only one I tell my secrets to. The only man who has ever loved me unconditionally, who has helped me heal when grief was becoming unbearable. Aiden kept me alive; he kept us alive. I will forever be grateful for him and the love and understanding and patience he showed me in a time I wanted to die. People grieve in different ways; we were able to grieve separately and together. We survived, because we had our love and each other and our children. They gave us hope on the days we felt hopeless. Losing Grace-Lynn was an unbearable loss for us all, the impact on our children was insufferable. We stayed strong as a family, mourning and healing, never to forget her, but do our best to live in a world without her here keeping her memory alive the best way we knew how.

Now, that we have grown old. Our babies have all grown up, having families of their own, and accomplishing their individual dreams. We could not have been prouder as parents. We survived, the un-survivable. All of us.

I sat on our porch, breathing in deep and exhaling as the Autumn wind blows through my long silver hair. I close my eyes, "I can feel you," I whisper, as I point my face to the sky. The evening sun was warm on my face, I heard laughter in the wind as it echo's, moving on through the wildflowers. Aiden walks out, joining me on the porch. I smile as he sits behind me. He wraps his arms around me holding me close, as the birds songs fills the silence around us. I close my eyes once more, taking in all the sounds of nature.

"Can you feel them? Can you hear them? They are all around us Aiden," I said to him. He kissed the top of my head, "Yes, my love they are," he said to me. When my eyes opened, Aiden is no longer behind me but standing just off to the side of our porch. His silver hair and those beautiful blue eyes, smiling at me. I look out towards the garden, and I see our wooden table, there in the grass. Abby, Jimmy, Calloway, Henry, and our parents, were all sitting at the table laughing and conversing in conversation. Our little Grace-Lynn was running around chasing the butterflies, laughing and giggling as she would attempt to catch on and then another. Her laughter was always contagious. Aiden, still standing off to the side holds out his hand, his eyes still smiling as they always did when he looked at me.

"Saoirse, it's time to come home my darling love," he said to me. Smiling, I close my eyes once more as I feel the wind blowing through my hair one last time. I then stand up, and take his hand in mind, he pulls me in close. Everyone at the table, staring at the two of us smiling just like our wedding day. I gently place my hand to Aiden's face, our eyes meeting once more, a youthful glow shining upon us both and I whisper softly to him, "I'm already home."


The End

# About the Author

Aubrie Sandness was born and raised in Washington state, She has always had a passion for reading and writing. She is a photographer by trade and now she is an Author. *In the Seasons of War* is her first novel. She currently resides in Washington state with her husband, their 2 children, along with their 2 Australian Shepherds.